CHAPTER 1
MY TIME

Peacefully awaking in a comfortable sea of pillows and blankets, I listened to the neighbor's lawn mower humming in the background. Happy birds chirped and welcomed a new day. Rolling over to adjust my pillow's position, I could barely make out the glowing red numbers on the alarm clock.

Hmm? 10:30 a.m.? Wow! Had I slept that long? Whoa, kind of late for a Monday. But there was no need to panic. No frenzied leaping out of bed for a quick brush-dress-eat scramble to the bus. None of that.

Why the carefree attitude? Had I transformed overnight into one of the "cool kids" who ditches school and plays Xbox in the basement all day? Nah! I was still the same old grade-conscious semi-nerd who lived for pop quizzes and book reports.

But I wasn't going to school that day. And no, it wasn't because of a heat wave, a teachers' workshop, or even a catastrophic power outage.

I wasn't sitting in a stuffy Kinney Elementary classroom because that particular Monday was the most glorious day of the year: the first day of summer vacation!

YEAAAAH! Good old summer vacay, baby!

Nothing but two and a half months of "me time" was in my immediate future. No alarms, no bus, no homework, and no crazy parents demanding to know EVERYTHING about school and homework.

It was time for kids across the country to unite in relaxation and breathe a collective sigh of relief that there would be no more Friday spelling tests or awful school lunches.

Sure, deep down, I loved school. But after almost ten months of academic stress and the pressure of chasing the honor roll, I needed to take the cerebral Ferrari back to the garage for an oil change and a new set of tires.

Summer vacation was MY time to relax, collect myself, and get reacquainted with my inner kid. And nothing says *inner kid* more than waking up at 10:30 a.m., pouring a giant bowl of Cap'n Crunch, parking myself on the couch, and watching *SportsCenter*. (*Comfy robe and bunny slippers optional.*)

The best part of summer was that I usually had the house all to myself. Mom and Dad both left for work early and got home late.

My sleep-loving older sister, Alexis, UNFORTUNATELY had lacrosse practice every day at 7:00 a.m., sharp. Mom drew the short straw and was responsible for waking the temperamental tigress and rolling her into the car each morning. *Soooooo sorry, Alexis. I'll sleep a few more hours for the both of us.*

YOU DON'T WANT TO WAKE **THIS** UP.

AND! To make my summer even more incredible, once Alexis got home, all she had time for was a quick sandwich and a glass of milk. She had to babysit the Quinlan kids across the street, and their mom wanted her there as soon as possible.

My parents loved the fact Alexis had a job, but everyone in my house (and on my street) was shocked to hear Alexis signed up to watch our town's four-headed monster, the Quinlan Quadruplets.

I REALLY don't know what she was thinking. Imagine trying to watch (and control) four eight-year-old boys who LOVED fighting, biting, inflicting pain, screaming, and general mayhem.

They were cute kids . . . from a distance. But you didn't want to get too close. The Quads were like a tornado of anarchy, breaking everything in sight and leaving behind a trail of destruction. However, this made them easy to find.

But for some reason, Barrett, Gerrett, Jerrett, and Merrett loved "Lexi! . . . Lexi! . . . Lexi! . . . Lexi!" and snapped to attention when she arrived. As soon as my sister showed up, Mrs. Quinlan's car screeched out of the driveway.

Alexis was getting paid a ton and even received weekly

"Quad Whisperer" bonuses because she was the only one who could control the four-headed beast.

So it was me, myself, and I, alone, all summer. AWESOME! But I had to be careful not to blow it. I knew fun-wrecking Dad would be keeping tabs on me. I could hear him now:

"You know, Jake, when I was your age, besides walking five miles to school, uphill, both ways, I spent all summer building forts, painting fences, and earning merit badges . . . BLAH . . . BLAH . . . BLAH!"

Once he realized my cushy setup, he'd stop at nothing

to derail my train of unsupervised fun. But I was too smart for Dad. No way was he ruining my freedom party. Dr. Phil was just starting a ten-part series on monster in-laws and the wives that hated them, and I couldn't miss that.

But I needed a plan. And fast.

First, I had to get some academics into the equation. That would buy me time and get Mom on my side.

Then, I needed to figure out a way to make money—without leaving the house. You can't watch TV sitting on top of the mini-fridge while you're mowing someone's lawn.

It didn't help that stupid Alexis was getting up at the crack of dawn, working out, AND making crazy money across the street. Plus, everyone thought she was SO brave. Ugh! Give me a break.

Of course, like I did everything else in my life, I found the answers to my all problems online.

Thank you, Google!

CHAPTER 2
CASH MONEY

The academic part was EASY! All I had
to do was visit my school's website.
They had billions of summer courses
available. I signed up for Social Media
Responsibilities, which was basically a
beginner's guide to the Internet:

SOCIAL MEDIA RESPONSIBILITIES DOS AND DON'TS

DO: Act like a responsible citizen when online

DON'T: Post more than one cat photo per day to
Instagram

DO: Refrain from name-calling and making others feel bad

DON'T: Create hundreds of fake Twitter accounts to make it seem like you have WAY more followers than your best friend

DO: Exercise caution; never post anything online you wouldn't want your parents or teachers to see

DON'T: Upload Vines of you and your pals toilet-papering the house of a boy who recently broke up with you*

*I call this one the Alexis Rule.

I was off to a great start. Social Media Responsibilities was going to be a cakewalk. But I was conflicted. Was I taking the academic coward's way out?

Absolutely! But then again, I'd never had the house to myself. Plus, this was MY summer vacation. Sometimes, in life, the path of least intellectual resistance makes more sense. Quickly getting over my fear of the easy A, I moved on to the second part of my plan: making that money.

Again, thank you, Internet. And Dad!

Every time we went to the beach, my father's swim trunks moved a few inches higher up his waist. I'm not saying he was trying to hide his giant gut . . . BUT . . . when your elastic waistband goes over your belly button, you might have a problem.

Not liking what he saw in the mirror, Dad decided to do something about it. Call it a midlife crisis, but he wasn't just going to stand by and get older, slower, and FATTER without a fight. Part of his new road to healthier living involved something called CrazyFit training. He asked if I wanted to be his partner, but there was no way I could do any of the exercises.

It's basically a workout designed by some guy who was obviously a construction worker. There are no weight machines or punching bags. But there are lots of sledgehammers, chunks of metal, giant thick ropes, and sacks filled with sand. I was more of a treadmill type of guy— CrazyFit wasn't for me.

One of the key components of any CrazyFit devotee's daily workout is a giant tractor tire. These things are humongous! They weigh hundreds of pounds and are used for flipping, rolling, slamming, and all sorts of heart-pounding abuse.

When Dad started looking for one to complete his garage gym, I helped him out. Within minutes of searching online, I found Howard Heavy Equipment: a farm-equipment store that was all too happy to give me an old tractor tire for free. The owner even delivered it to our house, no charge.

Too good to be true? Not really. It turned out I was doing them a favor. The store owner told me the disposal fees for these rubber monsters are HUGE. Instead of hauling them to the dump and being charged a ton of cash, he'd happily bring them to my house for FREE!

Nobody loves *free* more than my dad, and I got a new business idea.

It took me about five minutes to register a website and set up some Facebook and Twitter accounts. Before my father could say "Gee, Jake, did you do anything today?", Meathead Tires was live!

I received my first shipment of used tractor tires from the VERY thankful owner of Howard Heavy Equipment. And within minutes of posting the pictures, I got my first sale. Fifty bucks! *KA-CHING!*

But to make Meathead Tires really stand out, I needed to add a "cool" factor. Watching

Alexis come home every night exhausted after hours of nonstop Quad wrangling, I knew she'd welcome an opportunity for a break. If she agreed to roll the tires to and from the Quinlans' house, I'd allow the Quads to attack each one with paintbrushes and markers.

Alexis was only human. Even she needed a break from the constant running, chasing, and terrorizing. By turning the brothers loose creatively, she could get a few minutes of rest. Alexis sold it to Mrs. Quinlan as arts-and-crafts time for the boys.

It was brilliant! I now sold "customized" CrazyFit tractor tires displaying motivational workout phrases like:

NO PAIN, NO PAIN

FLIP ME ONE MORE TIME

IS THAT ALL YOU GOT?!

FEEL THE BURN!

MY GRANDMA HITS HARDER THAN YOU!

I was shocked. The Quads were good spellers and had perfect handwriting.

Before long, I cornered the used-tractor-tire market in the Baltimore metro area. I was the Great Oz behind the curtain of a CrazyFit empire, and I never had to lift a finger. No face-to-face contact. No small talk. No meeting potentially creepy and dangerous CrazyFit fanatics. And nobody knew Meathead Tires was run by a twelve-year-old kid with a cell phone and clueless parents.

Before long, I was making WAY more money than Alexis. She was going to be SO angry!

It had been a busy month. Time flew by. June was over, and Fourth of July weekend was right around the corner.

We always had a big cookout on the Fourth and invited relatives and friends over to celebrate. I knew it was the perfect time for Dad to start asking me questions. I couldn't WAIT to surprise him with my growing PayPal account, Meathead Tires' perfect Yelp score, and all my satisfied customers. He was going to be proud! Or so I thought. . .

CHAPTER 3
FIREWORKS

Independence Day was hot, humid, and miserable.

Dad was the only one brave enough to leave the air-conditioning. He fired up the grill and came back inside drenched. Gross! *Change your shirt, sweat beast!* Ordering Chinese food would have been so much easier. Nothing says Fourth of July like General Tso's chicken.

My friend Michael and I watched TV while Alexis and a few of her dorky friends gossiped in her room.

I hadn't seen Michael all summer. He was working for his dad, and on the weekends he traveled to compete in Tang Soo Do tournaments. I had to tell him all about my unsupervised summer of ME and Meathead Tires. Immediately he wanted one.

"Sorry, dude," I said. "No can do. They're fifty dollars each. No exceptions. BUT, if you show me some top secret martial-arts moves, preferably ones I can use to STUPEFY Alexis, I'll give you a discount."

"'Stupefy'? Do I look like Harry Potter to you?" Michael said. "Hold on, let me get my wand." He laughed and waved an imaginary stick.

HOW DID I GET HERE?

Lying on the couch with the AC blasting, we lazily channel-surfed for something to watch. The aroma of grilled onions, bacon, and beef filled the house. It was almost too much to handle.

When my mom finally announced lunch, we leaped up like a pair of wild hyenas. The Fourth feast was on!

Dad was INDEED a great grill master. Our flimsy paper

plates soon overflowed with bacon cheeseburgers, chili dogs, baked beans, and smoked sausage.

Acting as if they weren't dying of hunger, Alexis and her pals slowly drifted into the kitchen to have a look. Alexis's friend Becca pulled an "EWWW!" face. Politely, she asked my dad for something "gluten-free."

Immediately, shaking their heads in unison, like some synchronized, girl-posse bobbleheads, Alexis's buddies all started requesting the same thing:

"Yeah, Mr. Mathews, what Becca said: gluten-freeeeeeeeeeeeee!"

Like they knew what gluten was in the first place. My dad snarled something under his breath and pointed to a bunch of bananas sitting on the counter.

Alexis and her crew turned in a huff and stormed back to her room. *Excellent! More for me.*

My parents joined us at the table. For the first few minutes, there wasn't much talking. Just lots of finger-licking and mustard- and ketchup-squirting.

But soon enough, Mom had to know "everything" that was new with Michael and how his summer was going.

"Great so far, Mrs. Mathews. I love working for my dad. I'm learning so much about cars and engines," said Michael.

"Wow! Good for you, Michael. Way to get out there and get some real-world experience," said Dad, looking over at me.

"Yeah, Michael. GOOD . . . FOR . . . YOU!" I repeated with a mouth full of hot sausage. "But you know, Michael isn't the only working man around these parts."

"I forgot! Jake is doing an exceptional job of sitting around all day and eating us out of house and home," Dad announced to the table.

"That's not fair," interrupted Mom. "Jake is taking online classes this summer. And he is getting all As. I'm so proud of you, sweetheart. You're Momma's little scholar."

"'Classes'?" replied Dad. "More like ONE class. And I hope he gets an A. Alexis told me that course was a complete joke."

"Yup. My class *is* easy. Thankfully, it allows me more time to focus on growing my business," I said, slowly reaching into my pocket and pulling out my latest PayPal account summary.

It was the moment I'd looked forward to since the start of summer. Sliding the piece of paper across the table, I prepared for a tidal wave of shock and admiration.

Gazing at the transactions and account balance, Dad looked confused. Mom snatched the piece of paper from his hands.

"Jake Ali Mathews! WHERE did you get all this money?" Mom demanded.

"From sitting around all day on the couch. Right, Dad?" I said smugly.

"Jake . . . Now, be honest . . . Are you a hacker? I know you're good with the computer and everything. Please tell me you're not one of those cyber criminals who steals money from old ladies," pleaded Mom.

"No! I am a businessman," I said proudly. "And, unlike all of you, I don't just have a 'job.' I built an EMPIRE!"

"What are you talking about?" insisted Dad.

"I'm talking about Meathead Tires! Haven't you noticed the huge, multicolor, hard-to-miss tractor tires behind the house?" I asked.

All I got was blank stares from my parents. *How do they NOT see them?*

"I sell CrazyFit tractor tires online. That's what I'm doing this summer. And business is BOOMING!" I finally confessed. Standing up, I prepared for my hug and apologies.

"Are you kidding me?" said Dad, disappointedly throwing down his fork and sitting back in his chair. "More online nonsense? Come on, son. When are you going to get out from behind that computer screen? Like Michael is doing."

It felt like I'd actually been STUPEFIED by Lord Voldemort himself. I had no words. I couldn't believe what I was hearing.

"All you want to do is work and live in an online world of broad-bandwidth, mouse clacks, text mails, twerks, shelfies, and anonymous people," preached Dad.

"What are you talking about? I'm making WAY more money than Alexis. I thought you'd be proud of me?" I said, on the verge of tears.

*NOTE: I said "verge" of tears. I couldn't cry in front of my best friend.

"I AM proud of you. But I'm afraid you're not

experiencing life. You need to get out of this house more. It's great you're making money, but you're too young to be launching an 'empire.' It's okay to act like a kid sometimes," said Dad.

"So that's why you bought me *The Incredibly Risky and Dangersome Book for Boys*," I said sarcastically. "So I can learn how to act more like a kid? Do you really think making smoke bombs is a good idea? I burned my thumb, remember? I couldn't text for a week!"

"Yes, I do," said Dad. "That's what we did as kids. We played outside. All summer long. Left in the morning, went on adventures, and didn't come home until dinner."

Mom and Michael just sat there, saying nothing. *Awkward!* Maybe our "talk" should have been in private. *Too late.*

"So sorry, Park Ranger Mathews. The closest you come to 'getting outside' is watching bass fishing on TV," I said.

"Jake, all I'm trying to do is give you life advice. Now is the time to be experiencing the outdoors, trying new things, and acting like a kid," stated Dad.

One of Alexis's friends wandered into the kitchen and gazed longingly at the leftovers. Mom jumped up and forced her to take a few hamburgers and hot dogs back to the girls. It was a welcome distraction.

I didn't want to say anything I would regret—or that would get me in more trouble. But come on! One minute he wants everyone to work, and the next it's all about "being a kid."

"What do you think, Michael? What do you do for fun?" asked Dad, trying to lighten the mood.

"Ah . . . you know, the usual stuff," said Michael, looking down at his now empty plate.

"Like what? Besides lacrosse and martial arts. What about fun? Goofing-off stuff that isn't too serious," asked Dad.

"That's not fair. Don't drag Michael into your drama,"

said Mom. "He's trying to enjoy his lunch."

"It's okay, Mrs. Mathews," said Michael. "We go hiking sometimes. And, OH YEAH, next week, my dad and I are going to survival camp. It's going to be SICK!"

"Survival camp! Ha! Good luck with that." I laughed. "Hey, Dad, maybe we should go with them."

Dad looked over and gave me one of those "don't mess with me" looks, as if daring me to say another word. CrazyFit was one thing . . . like he'd ever dream of going to survival camp.

"Sounds AWESOME, Dad!" I laughed again. "You could show me how you lived off the land when you were my age. But unfortunately, I don't think you're allowed to bring your flat-screen TV and espresso maker."

Deliberately putting down his fork, Dad pulled his chair closer to Michael.

"Go ahead, Michael, tell me *everything* about survival camp!" said Dad.

CHAPTER 4
ALL ABOARD!

The more I heard about Camp Wild Survival, the WORSE it sounded. No running water. No beds. No food. NO WAY!

Michael and his dad signed up for the privilege of going out into the wilderness with nothing more than the clothes on their backs, a knife, and a compass. And apparently a death wish.

The purpose of the camp was to teach people how to survive in the wilderness. Okay. That's fine. I could see the value in that. But there is an easier solution: STAY OUT OF THE DARN WOODS! You'll never get lost that way.

According to Michael, the best part of the whole thing *(there's a best part?)* was the fact that Camp Wild Survival was being led by world-famous survivalist Thunder Banks.

THE Thunder Banks! You know . . . the dude with the funny accent who hosts all the survival shows on cable. He's ALWAYS eating something disgusting, climbing trees, being chased by bears, swimming in raging rivers . . . that guy!

"Ah, g'day, mate. It's your old pal Thunder here. Today, I want to talk about the nutritional value of witchetty grubs. Indeed, they might not look appetizing, but trust old Thunder—in a pinch, stuff a few of these beauties down your gullet and they'll save yer bacon. YUMMMM!"

Dad was mesmerized by what he heard. He even started to take notes. Nice try, Dad.

But his fake interest wasn't fooling me. There was NO WAY my dad would ever sign up for something like that. Right?

First, we had our yearly trip to Disney World coming up, and second, he wasn't that stupid. Who the heck wants to live in the woods for a week eating bugs and dreaming of TV?

Dad even excused himself and pretended to call Mr. Boyd to get more information.

As I watched him pacing around outside with his cell phone pressed against his ear, I felt sorry for him. It was SOOO hot out, and he was such a terrible actor. Thank goodness he had a steady job, because Hollywood wouldn't be calling anytime soon.

Sliding the patio door open, Dad strutted into the kitchen triumphantly.

"WE'RE IN!" yelled Dad as he slammed down his

notepad and looked at me for my initial reaction. *Okay, two can play that game.*

"NOOOOO WAY!" I exclaimed with fake enthusiasm. "Are you joking?! Please don't kid around about something so incredibly AWESOME!"

"Seriously. I got us in," said Dad. "We leave next week. Mr. Boyd said we can drive up with them—plenty of room, considering we can't bring any gear. So, get ready for the time of your life, young man!"

"Unbelievable!" I screamed, still going hard with the whole pretending thing. There was NO WAY I was going to give up first. I knew he didn't want to go. Dad was just waiting for me to crack and call for my mommy! It was like we were locked in an epic staring contest. Who'd blink first?

"DAD! I can't BELIEVE we're ACTUALLY going to meet the GREAT Thunder Banks!" I said with obvious insincerity. Clearly, I was mocking his interest in survival camp. But for some reason, he wasn't getting it.

"What? What's going on?" demanded Alexis as she stomped into the kitchen. "Thunder Banks?"

"Alexis," Dad gushed. "You're not going to believe it: Jake and I are going with Michael and his dad to Camp Wild Survival next week. We're going to be *hangin'* with Thunder!"

Looking confused, angry, and betrayed, Alexis tried desperately to figure out if this was all a joke. But there was no "just kidding" or "had you going there" coming from Dad. It was all too true.

"UNFAIR!" wailed Alexis. "I LOVE Thunder Banks. I watch all his shows: *Bushmen's Breakfast, Fire or Die, No Creek or Paddle, Surviving Naked* . . . Why Jake? He's terrified of the outdoors. Even the chipmunk under the front porch scares him. What a waste!"

"Sweetheart. You can't go. What about the Quads? The Quinlans need you," Mom reminded her.

"*Nooooo!* I forgot!" Alexis sighed as she slumped down in the seat next to Dad. "WHY must I be so GREAT at everything? Lacrosse, school, babysitting . . ."

"Overreacting, emotional outbursts, vandalism,"
I added.

"And the Quads love Thunder just as much as I do,"
said Alexis, burying her face in her hands.

Immediately, I saw my chance to end this
silly game once and for all. Because, as much
as Alexis and the Quads loved Thunder Banks,
Dad hated those four kids even more.

If they weren't picking his freshly planted flowers,
jumping in his neatly raked leaf piles, or bugging him for
rides on his lawn tractor, the Quads were always close by,
watching his every move. They were like four hyperactive
moths attracted to an angry flame.

"Alexis, you know, the
Quinlans think you're doing
an amazing job, right? I bet you
ANYTHING, if you go
over there and explain the

31

situation, they'll allow the Quads to come with us," I said.

After thinking about it for a few seconds, Alexis sprang up from her chair.

"You're right, Jake!" she agreed as she headed for the door.

"What just happened?" asked Dad. "There is NO WAY I'm paying for those four brats to go to survival camp. NO WAY!"

"Relax, honey. You have nothing to worry about," said Mom. "What mother in her right mind would entrust her four boys to Alexis at survival camp? Watch. Mary and Bob will politely tell Alexis no. But isn't it sweet she wants to take them?"

"Sweet? It's awful. I can't stand Huey, Dewey, Louie, and SCREWY. They'll ruin everything," whined Dad.

"Not a chance, Dad. We'll still have each other," I assured him. "I can't wait to battle the elements, live in the dangerous mountains, and search for food with you, PARTNER!"

Suddenly, Alexis burst through the front door. Out of breath, she could barely contain herself.

"They said YES! They SAID YESSSSSS!" she screamed, jumping up and down like some crazed teen at her first boy-band concert.

It was amazing to see the speed at which Alexis could get things done when she really wanted to. Even more amazing was the fact that Mr. and Mrs. Quinlan said yes without any information whatsoever about the camp.

Dad just stared at Mom. But before he could get a word out, a rumbling herd came bursting through the front door and barreling down the hallway.

The whole house shook as Barrett, Gerrett, Jerrett, and Merrett rounded the corner, bounced off the wall, and landed in middle of our kitchen.

Still overcome with emotion, Alexis pointed at Dad and said with tears of joy in her eyes, "There he is, guys, MY DAD! The one who's taking us ALL to Camp Wild Survival."

For little kids, the Quads were lightning quick, and they

pounced on Dad like he just hit a game-winning home run.
It was a mob scene. They all began to jump and chant
"THUNDER! THUNDER! THUNDER!"

Sitting back in my chair, I
watched Dad mouth to my
Mom, *I'm not paying for
them.*

He didn't have to worry.
The Quinlans were more
than happy to pay for
the Quads AND Alexis to
go to Camp Wild Survival. They
hadn't had a vacation in eight
years. That night Mr. and
Mrs. Quinlan booked themselves a trip to Cape Cod. They
couldn't have been happier.

Wow. Didn't see that coming!

CHAPTER 5
TOO FAR

There are times in life when you push your luck too far. Like the time I tried to jump three garbage cans on my bike . . .

As it turned out, two cans was my limit. As soon as I hit the ramp, I knew I had made a mistake. A trip to the hospital for a separated shoulder quickly reinforced that feeling. Since then, I've tried to stay away from any and all forms of death-defying.

Unfortunately, my stupid "who's going to blink first" contest with Dad had me feeling like I was once again headed up the three-can ramp of destruction.

To make matters even worse, and drive my anxiety even higher, Alexis printed out the Camp Wild Survival waiver:

MANDATORY—Must read, sign, and submit—MANDATORY

Camp Wild Survival Waiver and Release

a.) Camp Wild Survival ("CWS") is designed to be very difficult and EXTREMELY dangerous. You will be HUNGRY, exhausted, wet, miserable, and crying for your warm bed, BUT you will be in the company of world-renowned survival expert Thunder Banks. If you are not MAN (or woman) enough to accept these conditions, then PLEASE STAY HOME!

b.) Camper acknowledges that CWS is HAZARDOUS to their health and FULL of inherent risks such as: 1) wild-animal attacks—including Sasquatch encounters; 2) attacks from fellow campers dying from thirst or hunger (or both); 3) their own potential starvation or dehydration; 4) death by falling trees, tree limbs, and/or meteors; 5) extreme weather—heat, cold, humidity, ice, rain, fog, lightning, and/or a ridiculous combination of all; 6) poisonous plants, ticks, and too many venomous snakes to mention.

c.) Camper grants to CWS and its producers the absolute right to film, tape, and/or photograph, and otherwise use Camper's appearance and likeness in ANY WAY that CWS wants. We can make you a villain. Or portray you as extremely stupid. Also, CWS has the right to replay (over and over) any injury you might suffer. But who cares? You'll be on TV!

Finally, WELCOME to Camp Wild Survival! Get ready for excitement, FUN, and the adventure of a lifetime! And make sure to follow Thunder on Twitter @ThunderBanks.

Please sign:

_____

Name of Camper/Victim

DEATH WAIVER: I understand that I may die at CWS and do not blame, hold responsible, or assign ANY liability to the great Thunder Banks, or to Thunder Banks, Inc.

_____

Name of Camper/Deceased

After working out all the details with the Boyds, we planned to leave early Wednesday morning for the three-hour drive out to western Maryland.

Camp Wild Survival was being held on Black Lake at the foot of Big Savage Mountain. Oh, come on! As if I wasn't scared enough. Also, we received the official Camp Wild Survival rules in an email.

Basically, campers were only allowed to bring supplies that a typical hiker might pack for a day trip into the woods. This meant no tents, portable heaters, sleeping bags, stoves, food supplies, or anything else that would make our time at Camp Wild Survival remotely comfortable.

Standing in the rain, waiting for the Boyds, I looked over at my dad sipping on his morning coffee.

"Sooo . . . Camp Wild Survival! Excited?" I asked.

My dad turned to look at me and just stood there for a few seconds. With a BIG smile on his face.

"Excited? No. I think the correct word is *pumped*! Right? That's what the kids say, isn't it?" asked Dad.

"You're 'pumped'?" I gulped. "You're aware what's in store for us, right? Living in the woods, all the bugs, and, of course, the whole no-bathroom thing . . ."

"Oh yeah. I'm aware. And, like I said, PUMPED!" Dad laughed. "How about you? Not so *pumped,* are we?"

"Yeah, pumped," I squeaked out meekly.

No, I wasn't. But I'd never tell Dad that.

At 5:00 a.m. on the dot, Mr. Boyd's rumbling SUV arrived and blinded us with its massive headlights. The truck was huge. It had all sorts of storage racks and was jacked-up off the ground for extreme off-road action. Inside there was a cavernous backseat with enough room to lie down. I looked forward to a long nap.

Alexis wasn't so lucky. There was no relaxation in her future. She had to deal with four very excited little kids. And the Quinlans knew better than anyone the challenges associated with getting the Quads from point A to point B. So they graciously hired a van to take Alexis and the boys to camp.

Of course, Dad told the Quinlans it "wasn't necessary" and "don't be silly." But secretly, he'd crossed all his fingers and toes hoping he didn't have deal with a car ride from hell.

Throwing our bags in the back, I noticed Michael and his dad had just about the same amount of gear as we did. Not wanting to get in any trouble, I only packed extra socks, my Marmot pullover, two bottles of water, Pop-Tarts, and a multi-tool.

Dad brought a big hunting knife, matches, a sweater, some water, a portable headlamp, and some fishing line with a few hooks.

Alexis, on the other hand, wasn't what you would call a "follower of the rules." She'd never heard or read a rule she didn't immediately want to break.

Her preparation for Camp Wild Survival was a little different than ours. It took Alexis two days and multiple trips to the mall to

UM . . . NO THANKS.

strategically pack for herself and the Quads. She skillfully hid PowerBars, rain ponchos, bug repellant, hand sanitizer, whistles, magnifying glasses, rope, garbage bags, and other FORBIDDEN items, hoping to escape detection.

Also, the night before we left, Alexis told us her van would be making a few unscheduled stops along the road going into Camp Wild Survival. That's where she'd be hiding a few big green garbage bags full of extra supplies. Just to be safe.

Jumping out of the truck, Michael joined me in the backseat. It wasn't too long before both of us were once again headed to Snoozeville.

— — — — — — — — —

Waking up from a deep sleep is never fun. But the morning I arrived at Camp Wild Survival, I was both annoyed and depressed. Michael punched me in the leg to get me going.

Alexis and the Quads' van pulled up next to us as I stumbled out of the truck, trying to remember exactly what I was doing in the middle of the woods. Soon the

Quads were buzzing around the van like agitated hornets. Another part of Alexis's master plan was to have the Quads arrive wearing three layers of clothes. Who would notice?

Suddenly, doors were slamming, backpacks were flying, and my sister was trying to direct her angry swarm toward the sign-in tent.

"Dude, this is going to be SICK!" Michael assured me as he directed us toward a big tent filled with people. I wasn't sure I was ready for survival camp. And neither were my feet: They planted themselves firmly into the ground and refused to move forward. But one final shove from Michael had me moving in the right direction.

Dad and Mr. Boyd were deep in conversation as we waited in line with a few other families. It looked like there were about fifteen to twenty campers in total.

Camp staffers were everywhere, along with a whole bunch of guys who looked like bodyguards. They all wore black T-shirts and secret-agent earpieces. *I didn't know* the president of the United States was coming to camp.

Alexis had the Quads under control and easily negotiated the sign-in table, like she had done before at a hundred lacrosse camps.

Dad and Mr. Boyd handled our registration, and soon all the campers were waiting in the next line: Security Checkpoint Alpha.

As I waited to have my bag inspected, I turned my attention to the camp. It was pretty nice. Base camp, as we would soon learn to call it, was an old abandoned fishing site sitting right on the lake. There was a bunkhouse, a dock, a main cabin, and a few storage buildings.

The place was barren and judging from all the multicolor splotches that covered the neglected building, it was

HERE

evidently now used as a paintball battleground.

One thing that immediately caught my eye was the hard-to-miss, shiny, HUGE modern RV camper parked behind a storage building. HERE COMES THE THUNDER stretched from one end of the RV to the other in giant, bold, lightning-font letters. *I wonder who owns that?*

Off to the side of the RV was a row of tents, smaller trucks, multiple satellite dishes, and several port-a-potties. *All right, things are looking up!*

The security team emptied the contents of our bags and asked for our signed waivers. Alexis was next in line, and it was hilarious to watch her suddenly transform into a typical teenage "OMG" girl.

Security Guy: "Did you pack your own bag, young lady?"

Alexis: *"Yeaaaaahhhh.* I mean, like, who else *wooooould?"*

Security Guy: "Aha! What's this? I'm afraid we're going to have to hold on to your cell phone until the end of camp."

Alexis: *"Gawd!* Are you SERIOUS? *Reaaaally?* How am I supposed to see all the Snapchats from Becca's sleepover?"

Security: "Sorry. This is Camp Wild Survival. We have rules."

Alexis: *"Whatevs!"* (huffing and motioning for Security Guy to talk to the hand)

Security Guy: "Ah . . . Move along. Next!"

Two things: (a) The security guy confiscated Alexis's old crappy cell phone from about two years ago, and (B) He

didn't even check the Quads' bags. Brilliant!

Once all the campers cleared security, we were asked to stand in front of a whole bunch of TV cameras and wait for a greeting from Thunder himself. It was the moment Alexis and the Quads had dreamed about.

All of a sudden, the silence was shattered by squealing tires and multiple blasts from a car horn. A black SUV with tinted windows barreled down the road and came to a dusty stop. A guy in a suit and tie jumped out, followed by a kid and another guy. They looked very familiar.

"Good morning. So sorry to be late today! Please don't start without us!" yelled Donald Winston II as he haughtily strode past registration and security.

Behind Mr. Winston was DW III, dressed head-to-toe in brand-new survival gear. There was a third guy with them who I'd never seen before. He was dressed to match DW III perfectly—the exact same gear—but otherwise they looked nothing alike.

After a few minutes of discussion with the camp staff, Mr. Winston quickly hugged DW III and patted him on the head. Then he shook the other guy's hand and passed him something that looked like a large wad of cold, hard cash. After hopping back into the SUV, Mr. Winston was gone.

Seeing Michael and me standing there, DW III sauntered over to say hello.

"Well, well, well, if it isn't the Boss of Buzzkill and the world's Wildest Boy. I had no idea you two amateurs were even thinking about taking on Camp Wild Survival." Donald laughed.

"What happened to your dad, Donald?" I asked.

"He's a very IMPORTANT man," said Donald unconvincingly, looking around and noticing both of our fathers. "But I see your dads have the time. GOOD FOR THEM!"

"You're an idiot," said Michael. "Who's your friend over there?"

"Oh? That's Mr. Oren Longboat. Um, he's my dad's . . . COUSIN! Yes, cousin . . . on my grandmother's side," said an unsure Donald. "He's a member of the Seneca Nation and loves hunting and fishing."

"Your cousin?" I said. "More like your Wild Survival bodyguard. Pathetic!"

Suddenly, we were blasted with a loud sound track of rain sounds and poorly imitated cracks of thunder. It buzzed scratchily like one of those really bad haunted houses: not scary and kind of sad.

The camp's staff lined up in front of us, making a hunnel (human tunnel) all the way back to the door of the RV. Alexis and the Quads were going crazy.

Evidently, it's about to get THUNDERY up in here.

CHAPTER 6
SHOWTIME

Soon the cameras were in position. Giant light towers moved into place—even though it was late morning and perfectly sunny. And a guy with one of those black-and-white-striped clapper thingys jumped out the end of the hunnel and announced, "Thunder Banks intro . . . take one."

Behind us, an angry-looking older dude wearing a scarf (it was totally *not* scarf weather) and sunglasses sat in front of a monitor. He wore a hat that said BOSS, and everyone was crowded around him. They all looked nervous. He must have been very important. All of a sudden he screamed, "ACTION!"

I'll never forget the look of disgust on my dad's and Mr. Boyd's faces when the Thunder Banks circus kicked into high gear.

Like a boxer being led to the ring in Las Vegas for a championship fight, Thunder's entrance bordered on the ridiculous. C'mon man! This was survival camp, right?

Jogging down the hunnel and low-fiving the people on both sides, Thunder looked exactly as he did on TV: square jaw, flowing hair, and perfect-fitting khaki survival gear with tons of pockets.

As he stood before us, Thunder was all smiles, and he did a lot of that fake pointing at people. (I guarantee he had no idea who they were.)

"Ah, mate, great to see ya . . ."

"Looking good there, buddy . . ."

"Hey, guy . . . did you lose weight?"

Unfortunately, this made-for-TV moment was simply too much for the Quads to handle.

All their lives, the Quads had done exactly what they wanted. Why? Because they could. Mr. and Mrs. Quinlan had given up trying to correct their impulsive behavior a long time ago.

I'm not saying they're bad kids. Just the opposite. The Quads are actually very nice. They just know don't how to act around others. This explains why they were kicked out of public, private, AND home school—which I thought was impossible.

And even Alexis, the Quad Whisperer, couldn't keep them on their leash in the presence of their ultimate survival hero.

Breaking away from her control and easily blowing past security, the Quads quickly mobbed Thunder, who was now blowing kisses to imaginary fans.

"Cut . . . cut . . . CUT!" screamed the director as he threw down his megaphone in disgust.

"Thunder! Thunder! Thunder!" chanted Barrett, Gerrett, Jerrett, and Merrett as they hugged, pulled on, and basically mugged Mr. Banks.

Grabbing me by the shirt, a panicked Alexis gritted her teeth and barked, "I need your HELP!" as she dragged me out to assist her with the Quads.

"I'm SOOO sorry, Mr. Banks," said Alexis, head-locking Jerrett and Merrett, and attempting to gain control of the other two brothers.

I tried to pry Gerrett from Thunder's leg, but he had a really good grip.

Forcing a smile, as I'm sure he thought the cameras were still rolling, Thunder assured us it was okay.

"No worries, mates!" said Thunder. "And who are these cheeky monkeys?"

Immediately the angry-looking, scarf-wearing guy came running out and introduced himself as Sidney Powell, the director of all of Thunder's TV shows, camps, and appearances.

"These MUST be the Quinlan Quads. Even better than I expected," said Sid.

As Alexis and I tried to calm the Quads, who now—for some unexplained reason—were rolling around in the dirt and viciously fighting each other, I got a closer glimpse of the real Thunder Banks.

"Crikey, Sid! I said 'no kiddos,' mate! I thought we went over this? You know how I feel about ankle-biters," said Thunder, rolling his eyes and looking annoyed.

"Thunder, I understand, but think about it . . . These kids are TV gold," said Sid. "Cute. Quadruplets. Rough-and-tumble. They're rascals! The audience will eat them up!"

It looked like Thunder was about to go "full tantrum" and storm back to his RV. Sid tried to calm him down.

"Thunder, baby, you know I love you, right?" Sid assured him. "And I'm only telling you this because I care . . . Our latest viewer research shows that, for some unknown reason, you are extremely disliked by women ages nineteen to forty-nine."

"Mate! Who cares?" Thunder said. "My shows rank number one, number five, number eight, and number nine on the Extreme Outdoor channel. The Yanks can't get enough of ole Thunder Banks! I'm everywhere."

"And that's fantastic. But if you ever want to make the jump from cable to network, women need to love you. And right now, they don't," explained Sid.

"I LOVE HIM!" interrupted Alexis as she stepped forward to defend her idol.

"See, Sid? She loves me!" Thunder laughed.

"You must be Alexis," said Sid.

"Yes, sir. And once again, I am SO sorry about the Quads. They also *really* love Thunder," said Alexis.

"Great to hear," said Sid. "Hopefully we can film some spots this week featuring Thunder working with the Quads. They'll be perfect for promoting Thunder's new fall lineup."

After three more takes, Thunder finally nailed his entrance. The smoke machines added a lot.

Sid introduced himself to the rest of the campers and reminded us that the cameras would be rolling all week.

They weren't taping an actual show, just looking for short segments to use online as part of Thunder Inc.'s promotional campaign.

Finally, it was time to hear from the man himself. Requesting some privacy from the cameras, Thunder asked us to join him sitting on the ground as he gave us an overview of the week ahead. It was pure Thunder.

"First, I want everyone to know how *pumped* I am for Camp Wild Survival," gushed an enthusiastic Thunder. I snuck a glance at Dad. He was smiling.

"Everyone needs to keep in mind, this camp is for real," warned Thunder Banks. "Glorious Mother Nature is not cruel, but she doesn't tolerate fools. During this camp, you will be scared, and maybe even terrified. But that fear is natural. Don't hide it. It could save your life."

Wow, this turned serious awful quick. I liked it a lot better when it was all rascally Quads, lights, cameras, and smoke machines.

"I want everyone here to be extra-careful this week.

You can't stray to the dark side," cautioned Thunder. "The dark side of fear is panic. And in survival situations, panic kills! My job is to teach you just enough to conquer your panic and keep you alive."

I looked over at Dad, and suddenly he didn't appear to be quite so "pumped" anymore.

"Mr. Banks, sorry to interrupt, but I believe my father informed your staff about my allergies?" asked DW III.

"Hey, Sid, is this the kid that's afraid of snakes?" asked Thunder, pointing at DW III.

Sid came running up and whispered something in Thunder's ear. Thunder once again looked annoyed.

"Yessss, I'm aware. There's really nothing to worry about. There are only little baby snakes in these woods, sonny. BUT! Maybe later I'll tell everyone about the time I

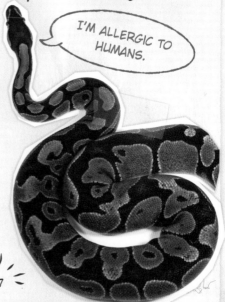

I'M ALLERGIC TO HUMANS.

was on a mission in the wilds of Borneo. I didn't have any rope, so I used a colony of pythons to hold together a bamboo raft . . . Luckily, their vice-like grips kept my vessel seaworthy, and I sailed down the river to safety," bragged Thunder as he stood up and started to ridiculously act out the scene.

Mr. Boyd laughed loudly.

"Something funny there, mate?" asked Thunder, looking at Mr. Boyd.

"No . . . no . . . no . . . sorry! Scratchy throat," explained Mr. Boyd, pointing to his neck. "Incredible story, though!"

"You're right. It's a beauty. You know, there are still headhunters over there . . . but that's ANOTHER story entirely!" Thunder laughed.

As Thunder turned to speak to his staff again, Michael looked at his dad and shrugged in disbelief.

"Seriously? Way to ruin camp on the first day, Dad!" said Michael.

"I'm sorry, guys. That was rude," Mr. Boyd said quietly

to us. "But I couldn't help it. I thought he was kidding. Wasn't he?"

My dad just looked at me with a blank expression. I think we were both ready to leave at that point. And then it got worse.

"It's time to jump right in," announced Thunder, who was once again demanding everyone's attention. "And, this being survival camp, I think it's best if we start with a simple challenge: I want everyone to drop their fancy packs and step back across the yellow line."

Looking down at my feet, I noticed a large yellow painted line that ran all the way around the outside of base camp. It was the same kind of paint they use for football fields. This line separated the buildings, Thunder's RV, the bathrooms, and the cabins from the lake, the forest, the great, scary outdoors . . . and us!

"Here's the scenario," Thunder began. "You're hiking in the woods with NO supplies. You foolishly pushed your luck, and it ran out. Now you're lost and need to survive the night. HOPEFULLY a search-and-rescue party will find you in the morning. The goal is to STAY ALIVE!"

Alexis and the Quads were hanging on every word.

"That's it. Good luck. Let's meet up again tomorrow morning at zero seven hundred, when you'll be reunited with your precious backpacks," added Thunder as he turned and walked back to his RV, which was humming with heat and probably Wi-Fi.

I looked down at my bag on the other side of the line. It was so close. Maybe I could quickly snatch a Pop-Tart from the front pocket. As I sneakily reached for the zipper, one of the security dudes stepped in front of the bag and yelled, "NO SUPPLIES!"

Dad walked up from behind and tugged me away by the arm. "We got this," he assured me.

Immediately I suggested we find shelter in Mr. Boyd's large and very comfortable truck. No one liked that idea. Everyone wanted the REAL survival experience.

CHAPTER 7
GONE FISHING

Immediately Mr. Boyd took charge of our group. Under his leadership, we had nothing to fear.

Mr. Boyd was a former Army Ranger who served in Operation Iraqi Freedom. A man of few words, he knew a whole lot about hunting and surviving. My dad was more than happy to listen and follow his instructions.

"All right, guys . . . AND ladies," said Mr. Boyd, smiling at Alexis. "The first thing we need to do is find a spot for our camp and then work together on building shelter and a fire."

"That's NOT what Thunder recommends," interrupted Alexis.

"Yeah, Thunder Banks says you should ALWAYS try to find food if you're lost. Maybe we can hunt a cow or something cool like that," suggested Merrett Quinlan.

"Remember that time Thunder parachuted from space and landed on top of that freezing glacier?" gushed Jerrett.

"And what's the first thing he did?" asked Alexis.

"He trapped a musk ox!" screamed the Quads.

SERIOUSLY?

"Yup. Exactly! He barbecued the ribs and slept inside its gutted body to protect himself from the cold," said Alexis, looking at Mr. Boyd with disbelief. "No disrespect, sir, but Thunder Banks is on TV. Obviously, he's an expert."

"Yeah . . . about that. He's DEAD wrong," stressed Mr. Boyd. "Kids, your body can last weeks without food. But in some challenging survival situations, you won't live twenty-four hours without water. And if it gets cold enough, you won't last the night without fire and shelter."

"I'm going with Mr. Boyd on this one, Alexis," I said.

"Yeah, honey, it makes the most sense," confessed Dad.

The Quads were very disappointed that musk ox-hunting was off the table.

We found an ideal campsite up against some boulders at the foot of Big Savage Mountain. Mr. Boyd thought the spot provided the best protection from the wind, and told us the rocks would give off heat during the night to keep us warm.

"How's a giant rock going to keep me warm?" asked

Merrett. "Thunder always has his portable wood stove."

"Excellent question," said Mr. Boyd. "Without getting too technical: Due to the changes in temperature during a diurnal heating cycle, coupled with the inherent thermal properties of igneous rock, the boulders will act like a giant heat sponge and continue to radiate warmth into the night."

Merrett looked around, trying to see if he was the only one who didn't understand the science lesson.

"Way to go, Dad, that wasn't technical at all!" Michael laughed.

"Really? I tried to keep it simple," explained Mr. Boyd. "Merrett, think of the rock as a giant potato that you put in the microwave for a few minutes. It stays hot after you take it out, right?"

"I don't know. We're not allowed to use the microwave anymore," replied Merrett.

"Poor Gizmo the goldfish. All I was trying to do was warm up his water for him," added Jerrett.

After a few more examples, the Quads and Alexis reluctantly agreed. Then Mr. Boyd assigned everyone a task, and we were off and running.

Interestingly, as soon as the challenge began, I had seen DW III and Mr. Longboat sprint to the edge of Black Lake and jump into a canoe. They paddled out to a tiny island about thirty yards offshore.

Within a few minutes, smoke had begun to rise from the island. Somehow I doubted DW III had anything to do with it.

It didn't take too long for my group to find enough branches, logs, and bark to make a decent-looking shelter. It helped—a lot—that the Quads were wood-collecting machines. They were like four tiny beavers in a rush to build their dam.

Michael, Dad, and I just did what we were told. None of us knew anything about "surviving." All we wanted was to be warm and dry.

Once the shelter was ready, Mr. Boyd asked if anyone was interested in learning how to start a fire. Everyone was, so we all took a seat.

"It's easy. Take out your very own Lightning Strikes survival matches, available for purchase at Thunder Banks. com!" screamed Barrett Quinlan.

"Or a magnifying glass to focus the sun's light. That always works," offered Gerrett.

"But what happens when Thunder's matches are wet, or when he doesn't pack his magnifying glass?" quizzed Alexis.

"Never leave home without your Nor'easter survival torch. 'Have no shame in your game when the weather's lame . . . You'll always get a flame with NOR'EASTER'!" roared the Quads.

"Are you kidding? Using a lighter is part of Thunder's survival teachings?" asked Mr. Boyd.

"How else do you start a fire?" asked Alexis.

"There're literally dozens of ways. And NONE of the methods you just mentioned are practical survival techniques," said Mr. Boyd. "Do you think primitive man had lighters? Matches?"

"Ahhhh—no! No need. They had dragons—which are VERY cool, by the way—and we don't," said Alexis, annoyed by Mr. Boyd's lack of dragon knowledge.

A confused Mr. Boyd decided to let that one go.

"Before there were any matches or lighters, people used flint and steel, the bow-drill technique, the fire plough, or a two-man friction-drill technique," said Mr. Boyd.

"Oh yeah! I remember that one. The old hand drill. That was part of my scout training," said Dad.

"Great! You were a Boy Scout?" asked Mr. Boyd.

"No, not a Boy Scout. More of a Cub . . . I was a Cub Scout," murmured Dad.

"That's MY dad! Come on over here, 'cubbie,' let's do that secret handshake." I laughed.

Dad got all red-faced and embarrassed. But soon he was front and center demonstrating the proper hand-drill fire-starting technique—with Mr. Boyd's help, of course.

Everyone got a chance to try. You had to spin a long stick in between your hands on

MY DAD!!

top of a softer piece of wood. The spinning created friction, which was SUPPOSED to produce a hot spark. But the only things it produced for me were blisters and frustration.

After ten minutes, none of the kids could do it. It was impossible!

But to his credit, Mr. Boyd patiently worked with us to improve our technique, and eventually everyone was able to start a fire without a lighter, matches, or a dragon.

With lots of the afternoon still left, and our fire and shelter looking good, we had some free time. Alexis and the Quads ran off to hunt "big game," and Michael and Mr. Boyd went for a hike.

"Hey, Jake. Look what I've got," said Dad, holding up a long, tangled fishing line with a hook on the end.

"Where did you get that?" I asked.

"I snuck it into camp. Let's go try to catch some fish," suggested Dad.

"Absolutely. We'll be heroes if we can bring back dinner," I said.

"My thoughts exactly," said Dad.

"But what about bait?" I asked.

Dad had that covered, too.

Reaching into his other pocket, he pulled
out a smashed-up jelly doughnut. Evidently, while Michael
and I were sleeping, our dad secretly stopped by the
doughnut shop. *Thanks for sharing!*

But without a pole, it was really hard to cast the
chunk of doughnut far from shore. Finally, Dad had a
lightbulb moment and tied a small rock just above the hook.
Bingo! Now our fried sugar-filled treat flew through the
air directly into the fish-infested waters.

EMPTY CALORIES!

WHAT, NO
SPRINKLES?

But after a few dozen tosses and no bites, we decided to just let the doughnut sink to the bottom of the lake and wait. Dad tied the other end of the line to his finger, just in case.

We both stretched out on the bank of the lake to relax. It was the first time in a while that Dad and I had really talked. He told me all about work—and also mentioned how impressed he was with Meathead Tires.

That was great to hear. FINALLY!

Suddenly, Dad's hand was almost ripped from his body. Something huge was at the other end of the line. And it REALLY loved doughnuts. Dad jumped to his feet and started pulling as hard as he could.

"Oh yes! We got one, Jake!" he

TREAT YOSELF!

shouted.

"That's AWESOME!" I said. "Go slow, don't yank the hook out."

Slowly but surely, Dad began to reel in the beast. Then we could see the outline of a BIG fish in the shallower water. Splashing and fighting, the fish resisted at every inch.

Our dinner was almost to the shore when the line snapped. It was over. Mr. Fish raced back to the deeper, darker water of Black Lake.

Dad and I just looked at each other.

"That was incredible!" screamed Dad.

"I KNOW, right?" I answered.

"We have to do more of this when we get home. Wow. Really gets the heart pounding," said Dad, exhausted and out of breath.

Just then, another voice joined the conversation.

"Nooooo! So close on that one, Mr. Mathews! Bad luck," shouted DW III from his tiny island fortress.

We looked up to see Donald sitting on a rock with his shirt off and sunglasses on. In the background was his campsite. Mr. Longboat had several large fish skewered on sticks cooking over an open fire . . . right next to a perfectly constructed lean-to shelter.

"Taking a break, Donald?" I asked sarcastically.

"Not really," yelled DW III. "My cousin wouldn't let me do anything. He's AMAZING! And to think I never wanted to go camping. So much fun!"

We'd heard enough. With the reality of no dinner setting in, Dad and I decided to head back to camp.

"My apologies . . ." DW III laughed behind us. "Please don't think I'm rude, but we have a strict dress code on Donald Island. If you can both find shoes and a dinner jacket, I'll have you over for a meal."

When we got back to camp, the Quads were sitting around the fire talking to Michael and Mr. Boyd. But Alexis wasn't there.

73

"What happened, guys? No luck cow hunting?" I asked the Quads.

"We almost had one . . . but Jerrett made too much noise and scared it away," whimpered Barrett.

"Shut up, Barrett!" shouted Jerrett. "How are we supposed to catch a cow without milk, you jerk?"

"Whoa, fellas! No need for that," I said. "Where's Alexis, anyway?"

"She went for a walk. She told us she needed 'alone time,' so we have to wait here," said Merrett.

An hour later it was almost dark, and Alexis still wasn't back. The Quads were hungry and tired, and Dad started to worry.

"Geez, it's the first day of camp, and ALREADY Alexis is driving me crazy," said Dad.

"She'll be fine," said Mr. Boyd. "Obviously, she watches a lot of survival TV . . . which, on second thought, may or may not be a good thing."

Suddenly, there was rustling in the bushes, and Alexis

burst through the vegetation and somersaulted into camp.

The Quads went nuts and mobbed her as if she'd been gone for years.

"You are CORRECT, Mr. Boyd. I do watch lots of survival TV," said Alexis as she stood up, covered in dirt, twigs, and Quads. "But in this case, it is indeed a GOOD thing. Behold, Quinlan Quads, I bring your glorious FOOD!"

Alexis reached into her pockets and started showering the brothers with protein bars and gummy bears. The Quads wouldn't be going to bed hungry, after all.

"I think you will agree, a good survivalist is ALWAYS prepared," gloated Alexis.

Mr. Boyd had no words.

CHAPTER 8
ANTLER TALES

Getting up at the break of dawn wasn't hard. I was already awake. And wet. And cranky! And completely OVER Camp Wild Survival!

Yeah, building a shelter, fishing, and bonding with Dad was fun. But the whole sleeping-under-the-stars thing was overrated.

First, there were no stars. Just rain. All night it felt like the ocean was being dumped on my head.

Second, my dad snores. So does Alexis. And the Quads ALL talk in their sleep. They have full-blown conversations—with each other. CREEPY!

Mr. Boyd had to double-check and make sure our fire was completely out before we left for the morning meeting with Thunder. *Come on!* It was STILL pouring, and our wood was submerged in a

puddle. Even Smokey the Bear would say "You're good."

Walking out of the woods, I could see that a few other campers beat us to the rendezvous point. There was no sign of Thunder Banks or any of his staff.

Standing tall and in formation just outside the yellow line, the Conley family from Delaware eagerly awaited the arrival of our host. They looked like a bunch of newly recruited soldiers for Thunder's Army.

I quickly figured out the Conleys were preppers. How did I know this dad and his two kids were preppers? The bumper stickers on their minivan gave them away:

WE PREP, YOU DIE; PREPPERS: LIKE HIPPIES, BUT WITH GAS

MASKS; THE BOY SCOUTS GOT NOTHING ON US; HAPPINESS IS RUNNING WATER IN YOUR UNDERGROUND BUNKER.

In case you didn't know, preppers are people who prepare for the world to end. Also known as "doomsday preppers," they buy years' worth of food and toilet paper in anticipation of some sort of disaster. Alexis watched a lot of prepper shows on TV. They usually came on right after Thunder Banks.

Next to the prepper family stood a husband-and-wife team from Washington, DC.

They were both doctors, and I had overheard them talking in the registration line the first day. Apparently, survival camp was on their bucket list. But after a night in the cold rain, I wonder where Camp Wild Survival ranks with cool stuff like swimming with sharks, standing on top of a giant pyramid, or going to the Super Bowl.

I didn't see DW III or his "cousin." And I also didn't see the team of three angry grandmas. *Boy, were they mad when they didn't get to chance to talk to Thunder* yesterday. Hopefully they've calmed down. A good soaking will take the sass out of anyone.

Slowly the camp staff and all the TV people started showing up. The lights were moved into place, and everything was ready for Thunder's morning appearance.

DW III finally made it, looking dry, cheerful, and well rested.

"WHAT . . . A . . . NIGHT!" bragged Donald. "There is NOTHING like getting back to nature and experiencing the wilderness. Who knew it would be so comfortable. The dreams I had!"

Oren Longboat rolled his eyes and looked away, shaking his head.

Finally, the door of the RV swung open. Here comes Thunder! In his pajamas?

With a cup of coffee in one hand and a softball-size muffin in the other, Thunder looked like he had just rolled out of bed.

But, man, that muffin looked GOOD! Its sugar crystals shimmered like small diamonds. And the oozing blueberries glittered like sapphires. *Geez, hunger really amps up my imagination.*

Speaking with the TV production guys, Thunder acted like we weren't even there . . . waiting . . . for him! IN THE RAIN!

Quickly, Sid nudged Thunder and motioned over to us. Snapping to it, and putting on a fake smile, Thunder jogged over and heartily greeted everyone: "It's a GREAT MORNING to be alive!"

No one responded.

"Wow. What a sorry-looking lot. Ghastly weather, ay? The Great Mother really wanted to put you through the wringer." Thunder laughed. "Did they tell you we're running slightly behind schedule?"

Sid joined Thunder on the other side of the yellow line.

"Yeah, we had a bit of a hiccup last night. The Grandma Team 'tapped out' and went home," said Sid.

"Apparently, they didn't know this was a survival camp. They thought it was going to be more of a lake cruise with a Thunder Banks meet-and-greet."

"Not to worry, I did get to spend some time with the old gals before they left. Signed their books, took a few photos . . . They were in heaven," said Thunder proudly.

"Just give us five, and Thunder will speed through wardrobe and makeup and be right with you," said Sid apologetically.

"And you can reunite with your backpacks. Sorry. I wanted you to experience raw nature and the terrifying reality of the bush firsthand. You're better for it. Trust me," Thunder assured us.

"Yeah, better for it. I'd be 'better' if I were sleeping in your sweet RV and drinking some of that hot coffee," my dad muttered under his breath.

Everyone started to laugh.

Twenty-five minutes later, Thunder appeared before us once again in a wrinkle-free khaki survival outfit. TV's greatest outdoorsman was about to get down to business.

Cameras rolled as we all sat under a giant tent. They served hot cereal and doughnuts and allowed us to change into dry clothes. Immediately, everyone was in better spirits. Even Dad.

"Okay. Let's start with some feedback from last night," said Thunder. "How'd it go? Any problems? From the looks of it, everyone could use a refresher course in shelter building."

Almost everyone complained about the rain and lack of food. Everyone except DW III. He smartly stayed very quiet.

"I don't want to sound paranoid, but I think there might be a giant swarm of bees living in the woods," said Dr. Jillian Andrews.

"Really?" asked Thunder. "You saw a swarm of bees?"

"We didn't see them,"

AND YOU THOUGHT FREDDY KRUGER WAS SCARY!

Dr. Jillian said. "But we heard them, all right. My husband and I were walking near the lake around dusk, and we heard this very loud buzzing sound over our heads."

"Crazy loud!" said a still-shaken Dr. Mike Andrews. "Then I remembered reading about Africanized killer bees in last month's medical journal. That's when I FREAKED OUT!"

"Africanized bees, huh?" said Thunder. "AFRICA . . . the Plateau Continent. A big-game paradise. A land of extreme beauty and danger." He turned and walked away, completely ignoring Dr. Mike.

"She's a real stunner, Africa. Reminds of the time I was on patrol in Namibia, smack in the middle of the mighty Kalahari Desert. No food, no water, and no hope," said Thunder, lost in his own thoughts. "It was looking grim until SUDDENLY—"

"Ahem! AHEM!" Sid coughed and stared at Thunder in disbelief.

"What? Oh, right. I should shut my gob. That's a story

for another time," stammered Thunder. "Don't worry, doctor. My guys will check it out. I HOPE it's a swarm of killer bees. Then I'll show you how I survived a week in Guyana by eating ONLY killer-bee honeycombs. They're like kittens if you know what you're doing."

Getting back on track, Thunder let us know that hunting-and-gathering training was the focus of the day. Since, OF COURSE, food was the most important aspect of surviving in the wild. I didn't even have to look. I could imagine the scowl of disapproval on Mr. Boyd's face.

But it did sound like a lot of FUN. We were going to learn about tracking animals, setting all kinds of traps and snares, and even skinning game and how to best to prepare a fresh kill. AWESOME!

Thunder's staff was also going to review some "gathering" fundamentals, like identifying edible plants and "safe" mushrooms.

But he hoped they wouldn't waste too much time on that "unimportant" stuff. We didn't need to rely on greens to stay alive.

"Basically, we're all animals. We need meat to live. It's full of energy and protein. And can mean the difference between life and death in the bush," stressed Thunder.

"Yeah, Thunder! YOU the man!" screamed Gerrett Quinlan.

"Ah, good on ya, young man! I know YOU'RE a survivor." Thunder applauded.

"Meat rules!" screamed Merrett. "Like the time you captured that moose in Finland!"

"THAT WAS EPIC!" answered Jerrett, turning to the rest of the campers. "Mr. Banks snuck up on a moose and wrestled it to the ground by its antlers."

"Sid, can you believe it?" roared Thunder Banks. "Real Thunder Maniacs. Dig a hole and bury me, it just doesn't get better than this!"

TASTES LIKE CHICKEN?

Hold on! I thought. *Thunder had hand-to-hand combat with a moose? I don't remember seeing that.* I immediately turned around to Alexis for confirmation.

"Oh yeah! He REALLY did," Alexis assured me in a whisper as she leaned forward, not wanting to interrupt the Thunderfest.

Oren Longboat raised his hand to ask a question.

"Yes, sir?" acknowledged Thunder.

"You hunt moose by wrestling them to the ground?" asked Mr. Longboat.

"Not every time," said Thunder, getting a little defensive. "And I don't recommend it. But, remember, there are no rules when it comes to survival."

"I've hunted for most of my life," interrupted Mr. Boyd. "I'm curious to know how you got close enough to the two-thousand-pound, eight-foot-tall animal to grab it by the antlers?"

"Moose have terrible eyesight," answered Barrett. "EVERYONE knows that. Plus, Thunder bathed the night before in moose droppings to cover his own human scent."

Gross! Scratch moose hunting off the list.

"Then he held two large branches over his head to look like his own antlers," continued Barrett. "The moose just thought Thunder was one of his friends. He was able to walk right up the moose and GRAB him!"

"There you go," Thunder Banks said pompously. "My biggest fans know the answer. And they're better survivalists for it. In case you want to see it for yourself, it's on YouTube. Season four, episode six."

I wasn't the only one who had doubts about the story.

"Too bad there aren't any moose here in Maryland, or I'd give you a real live demonstration," added Thunder.

"I'd love to see your technique," said Oren Longboat.

"Maybe you will someday. Or maybe you'll find yourself in a survival situation that requires you to think outside the box like I do," said Thunder as he slowly got up from his stool. The cameramen rushed in for close-ups, anticipating a classic Thunder speech.

"Remember, I'm a regular guy. Just like you," Thunder Banks began. "I wake up every morning and put on my ergonomic, UV-protected survival trousers with Kevlar-reinforced pockets one leg at a time—"

"CUT! Thunder, you need to be pointing at the pants AND looking into the camera at the same time," shouted Sid. "It's only good product placement if the audience can soak up your sincerity. Sell them with your eyes! You're better than that."

While Thunder and Sid argued about which angle best highlighted his new line of wilderness apparel, the rest of us were dismissed and sent off to hunting and gathering training.

Reluctantly I picked up my backpack and walked toward the woods. I just hoped they weren't going to give Alexis and the Quads any sort of weapons. Those guys had hunting on their minds and who knew what they'd consider "big game." I had put on some weight that summer . . .

CHAPTER 9
GOING TRIBAL

After breaking into smaller groups, we spent the rest of the morning learning from Thunder's staff of expert outdoorsmen.

Of course, hunting was the longest and most detailed of the sessions. I was amazed to find out what you could eat if you really had to. Squirrel? Possum? You bet! Remember, we're talking survival. If I had a choice, it would be pizza.

SAY WHAT NOW?

We learned that the key to any good hunt is thinking like your prey.

What would Mr. Squirrel do in this situation? Well, if I were him, I'd stay in my tree until the hungry-looking guys walking around below gave up and went home.

The best part of the day was the traps-and-snares demonstration. But Dad almost broke his fingers when the rock he was using in his deadfall trap fell on his hand. *OUCH! Looks like they didn't cover that stuff in Cub Scouts.*

I could tell Dad was growing more and more frustrated with each hour. For a guy who claimed to love the great outdoors, Dad just didn't have the skill set to be a mighty hunter.

Besides almost breaking his hand, he didn't want anything to do with the skinning and meat-processing tutorials.

Apparently, the camp staff had been busy the day before, collecting local roadkill for us to practice our newly learned field-dressing techniques.

YES, it was disgusting. But nothing our ancestors

didn't have to do every day. We learned the H and I skinning patterns, so once our prey was caught, we could quickly get it into the pot. Dad was having NONE of it.

"Here you go, Mr. Mathews. A nice woodchuck for you to practice on," said Instructor Tom. "I suggest field dressing him using an H pattern."

"No thanks! What time does the gathering instruction start?" asked Dad.

So Dad got an F in hunting. He quickly found out that gathering wasn't much better.

"We are fortunate to be camping here in an abundant region of Appalachia," advised Instructor Dave. "Here, dandelions, wild violets, cattails, leeks, stinging nettles, and pokeweed sprouts are plentiful. And delicious!"

"Did you hear that, Dad? Pokeweed sprouts. YUM! I think they'll go perfect with a pine-needle sandwich," I said.

"Keep it up. I'm about to *poke* you right in the eye,"
said Dad. "Next!"

Finally, we made it over to the fishing tutorial. That
was more Dad's speed. For some reason, catching, filleting,
and eating a fish didn't seem to bother the Big Guy as
much as carving up a woodland creature.

It turned out Black Lake was full of tasty fish. We
soon learned how to make hooks from animal bones and
sticks. And who knew that shoelaces would make excellent
fishing lines in a survival situation?

Soon we were experimenting with new types of bait,
finding large branches to use as poles, and learning exactly
where all the "giants" were hanging out.

Dad was in fishing heaven—happy, smiling, and not
worried about snaring raccoons or figuring out which
innocent-looking mushroom could kill ten men. It was all
brown trout, smallmouth bass, walleye, bluegill, and tiger
muskies.

But Dad's lakeside relaxation was soon interrupted

by a loud air-horn blast. That was the signal for another
Thunder meeting back at base camp.

Returning to the tent, we found Thunder standing
next to a huge scoreboard. On the board were the names
of each group/family, along with a new tribal name.

SURVIVAL CHALLENGE SCOREBOARD

FAMILY NAME	TRIBAL NAME	SCORE
THE MATHEWSES AND THE QUINLANS	BALI AGA	0
THE BOYDS	PALAU	0
DONALD WINSTON AND OREN LONGBOAT	HIMALAYA	0
THE ANDREWSES	BIG SUR	0
THE CONLEYS	DENALI	0

LIKE US ON FACEBOOK   @THUNDERBANKS

"As you can see, you have each been newly assigned a
tribal name. And in the spirit of survival, I've decided to

make the rest of camp one big competition," announced Thunder.

"Your tribe will be awarded points for how you do in the upcoming challenges," he continued. "At the end of camp, the tribe with the most points will win something very cool. Trust me, you want to win!"

The Quads and Alexis started high-fiving and getting all excited.

"You've all received hunting-and-gathering training from some of the top survivalists in the world this morning. It's now time to put those skills to the test," said Thunder.

"At the sound of the air horn, each tribe will have four hours to hunt, gather, and catch as much food as you can. A staff member will monitor your progress. At no time shall you speak to them or ask for help," warned Thunder. "Any questions?"

"Yeah, how does the scoring work?" inquired prepper dad Mr. Conley.

"Does it matter what we bring back?" asked Mr. Boyd.

"Of course it matters. Meat is king! I won't be impressed with a bushel of clover. But a grizzly bear? That'll score mega points," suggested Thunder.

FEELING LUCKY, PUNK?!

"Grizzly bear? Where does this guy think he is?" asked Mr. Boyd, turning to my dad.

We had ten minutes to prepare for the challenge. So Dad decided to call our new tribe together for a quick meeting. Right off the bat, Alexis had a problem with Dad's plan.

"Okay, Tribe Bali Aga. Hope you don't mind, but I'd like to take the lead on this challenge," offered Dad.

"You're asking us?" questioned Alexis. "Great leaders don't ask permission. They just do it."

"Relax, Alexis," I said. "Dad is being diplomatic. Of course he will lead us into this food/survival battle."

"Thank you, Jake, for the vote of confidence," said

Dad. "And if YOU"—he pointed at my sister—"have a problem with me as team leader, we can have that discussion . . . along with a chat about your cell phone charges from last month."

"NO! No problem at all. You da man!" agreed Alexis.

Dad's plan was simple and predictable: Tribe Bali Aga would be fishing.

CHAPTER 10
THE HUNT

The air horn blasted, and the tribes raced out of camp.
Thunder cheered us on.

"Off to the hunt, you great warriors! I envy ALL of
you. Who knows what game lurks in this deep forest.
Free-range bison? Maybe an elk or two? I can't wait to
see your bountiful harvests," Thunder shouted from the
safety and comfort of base camp.

Dad could hardly contain his excitement when it
turned out we were the only tribe that wanted to fish.

Mr. Odom was our survival monitor. He was an older
guy with gray hair. But he still looked really mean and

tough. As he sat under a nearby tree with his notepad, I heard him mutter, "Oh gawd!" under his breath as my dad giddily discussed our fishing plans.

"Oh man! What luck! We're going to win for sure," Dad said as we quickly got to making poles and hooks.

BOO-YAH!

The Quads were assigned bait duty—which they loved! I swear, those kids are like gophers. Within minutes they dug a giant trench in the ground and were hauling out huge worms.

We quickly had three poles ready to go, worms the size

of small snakes, and a lake full of fish. It was Dad's dream scenario.

And when he caught that first trout, you'd think he had just won the lottery.

Jumping up and down with lots of *boo-yahs* and *that's what I'm talkin' about*s, Dad was like a kid in an unhygienic, bug-infested candy store.

Unfortunately, the frenzied excitement was too much for the attention-craving Quads to handle. They had been sitting patiently, watching me, Dad, and Alexis fish. But now they wanted in on the action.

"Mr. Mathews, can I have a turn?" asked Merrett as he walked up to Dad from behind.

"In a minute, guys. We really need to catch a few more. This is important," said Dad. "But, hey, in the meantime, we're DEFINITELY going to need more worms. And you four are the world's best worm catchers!"

"I don't want to be a worm catcher. I want to fish," said Jerrett.

"Yeah, me too," added Barrett.

"ALEXIS! Deal with that . . . ,"
Dad whispered, pointing to the
four troublemakers.

"Ah, come on, Dad. Let Merrett have a
turn," said Alexis.

You'd think she had just asked Gollum to
give up his Precious.

"Are you CRAZY?" said Dad. "I'm catching
fish! We're going to win this challenge.
I've never caught this many
fish in my life. This is
AWESOME. Give them your pole."

But before any of us
could decide who was going
to share their pole, the
first worm was thrown.
And then the second.
Followed by a handful of dirt.

Without warning, it was a full-blown Quad war.
I couldn't tell who was on whose side, or
if they were all fighting each other. But it
escalated quickly.

The dreamlike tranquility of Dad's fishing
scene was shattered by flying worms,
clumps of dirt, and four screaming kids
rolling around on the ground.

"ALEXIS! They are scaring the fish!" yelled Dad as a worm
splatted against his face.

Alexis dropped her pole and jumped right into the brawl.
Like a hockey referee, she desperately tried to separate the
wild brothers. Only the threat of being sent home brought
peace to our tribe.

Once the tears were dried and the *he started it*s were
over, Alexis sent the Quads

on a mission. Their punishment was to collect dandelions.

And after being completely bored watching our attempt at catching fish, Mr. Odom saw his opportunity for something more exciting. He volunteered to watch over the Quads as they journeyed into the woods on their weed hunt. But he missed all the action.

Before long, the Mathews family was no longer fishing: We were just catching.

It was crazy. As our handmade branch poles bent to maximum flexibility, we hauled in fish after fish. Dad was going berserk.

After a while, we lost count of how many we had. The Big Guy couldn't stop smiling and laughing. Alexis and I had never seen him so happy.

But two blasts of the air horn signaled the end of our fishing adventure. Wow, time had flown by, and now we had only thirty minutes to clean up and get the fish back to camp. That's when we realized the Quads had been gone for WAY too long. *Uh-oh!*

"Don't worry. They'll be all right. Besides, Mr. Odom is watching them. Remember?" said Dad. "What's the worst that could happen? I feel sorry for the mountain lion that thinks those four are an easy snack."

"DAD!" screamed Alexis.

"Kidding! They'll be waiting for us back at base camp," said Dad. "They're probably sitting cross-legged listening to another one of Thunder's ridiculous stories."

But he was wrong. Back at camp, the Quads were no where to be found. And it was time for tribal show-and-tell.

Thunder paced around impatiently, waiting to see what each tribe had brought back from its day in the woods.

Much to my surprise, Michael and his dad had nothing.

What? I couldn't believe it. They said their snares weren't working and they'd had no luck tracking any animals. Thunder looked overjoyed and even offered to give Mr. Boyd a private lesson later in the week.

The prepper family had a ton of mushrooms and other weeds. Thunder just shook his head and gave an *ew* face. He couldn't hide his dislike for "rabbit food."

Mr. and Mrs. "Doctor" also came up empty but let Thunder know they were really enjoying the fresh air. Thunder murmured "pathetic" as the couple tried to describe the "glorious" waterfall and rainbow they encountered on the other side of the lake.

"Unfortunately, you can't eat rainbows, Doctor," scolded an annoyed Thunder Banks. "Your team earns ZERO points."

Donald came over to have a look at our HUGE haul of fish.

"Holy moly. Did you leave any in the lake for the rest of us?" DW III laughed.

Thunder looked impressed. Dad was so proud.

"Okay! Good on ya, Bali Aga. Excellent job!" said Thunder. "At least someone around here is eating tonight."

"Yummy, Jake!" said DW III, rubbing his stomach. "Enjoy your boney fish and all their parasites."

"You must love them, too. You ate a bunch the other night!" I said.

"Disgusting! I didn't eat any. They're all for Mr. Longboat. Who knows what's in that water?" said DW III.

"If you don't eat fish, what have you been eating for last two days?" I asked.

"Aaah, nothing! Nothing at all. When you have a strong mind, hunger isn't much of a distraction," said Donald quickly, trying to change the subject.

The big clock in the tent showed ten minutes to go in the challenge and still no Quads. Also, Oren Longboat was missing.

"Where's your partner?" Thunder asked DW III.

"I have NO idea. That dude just kept running. After a

while I gave up and walked back," said DW III. "But hold on. I spoke too soon. Here he comes. Oh . . . MY . . . . GOSH!"

Oren Longboat stumbled clumsily out of the woods and into the clearing. Drenched in sweat, he was breathing heavily and looked exhausted—like a marathon runner who had just crossed the finish line.

BUT I can honestly say I've never seen a runner finish a race with a large deer slung over their shoulders. And this deer was very much ALIVE!

"I THINK we have a winner!" yelled DW III.

CHAPTER 11
FROZEN WITH DEER

The buzzing from the campers and the loud "CRIKEY!" from Thunder terrified the poor deer. It tried desperately to wriggle free. But Mr. Longboat had tied its hooves with vines and had a REALLY good hold on its head and hind legs.

Oren Longboat gently laid the deer at Thunder's feet. A crowd of staffers, TV production people, and basically everyone else in camp gathered around.

"So what do you think, Thunder? Is it safe to say Tribe Himalaya is the winner?" gloated DW III.

"Amazing. Well DONE, Oren! And that's exactly how I

like my venison!" joked Thunder, kneeling down to admire the animal.

Oren Longboat explained how he had used a basic circle snare to catch the deer, but it had taken hours to haul it back to camp alive.

"Mate, I have to ask: You have a knife—why didn't you just field dress it in the woods?" asked Thunder. "Packing out sixty pounds of meat would have been a lot easier than a live deer."

"Why? I did it for you, Mr. Banks," said Oren Longboat.

"For me? I'm flattered. But I'm also STARVING. And deer is such a delicious treat. Let's fire up the barbie and get this thing grilled," said Thunder.

"No, no, you don't understand. I brought this deer back so you could demonstrate for all of us," said Oren. "I'm sorry it's so small. Obviously, it's nowhere near the size of a moose. But it's got huge antlers, which will be easy for you to grab."

NOOOO WAAAYYYYY! This should be good! Be careful what you wish for, Thunder Banks.

Quickly Sid and the whole production team were in a panic. Thunder started to go a little pale.

"WAIT a minute!" said Sid. "What do you mean? If you think Thunder is going to give a live deer-wrestling demo without all the precautions, back-ups, and safety measures in place, you're crazy."

"Why not?" Oren Longboat said. "This is a 'survival situation,' after all. If Thunder can take down a moose, surely this tiny deer should be piece of cake. I can't wait to see your technique."

"I'm *also* intrigued by this hunting method," said Mr. Boyd, adding fuel to the Thunder-humiliation fire.

"Show 'em how it's done, Thunder!" screamed Alexis.

Within seconds, Oren Longboat had begun to cut the vines holding the deer's hooves and stood over its back, barely holding on to the antlers. It looked like he was ready for his lesson.

"Okay, Thunder," called Oren. "Are you all set? I'll let him go, and you show us how it's done!"

The deer might have been small, but he was ANGRY! He looked like one of those cartoon animals—the ones with steam coming out of their noses.

LESSON?

Sensing immediate danger, everyone in the crowd immediately took a few steps back. Everyone . . . except Thunder.

He was too scared to move. Thunder was frozen—like a deer in headlights. *Irony alert!*

But just before things got interesting, Thunder's team of very burly survivalist instructors jumped in and formed a human shield around their trembling boss.

Realizing he was out of the danger zone, the color returned to Thunder's face. He immediately flipped the switch into full-blown TV-Thunder mode.

"Everyone, out of way! Get back. Let me at him. Turn that puny deer loose," shouted Thunder—who was NOT trying very hard to fight his way through his security team.

Sid easily pulled Thunder away from the chaos.

"Sorry, Thunder. No can do. Remember what your doctor told you?" Sid reminded him. "His strict instructions? Remember? Absolutely no overdoing it this week."

"Ah, Sid, come on! It's a DEER. Just this once," pleaded Thunder. "I'm READY, Oren. Watch closely how I grab the antlers and then sweep the legs. Is anyone recording this?"

With his suspicions satisfied, Mr. Longboat yanked the deer by the antlers and pointed him in the opposite direction of Team Thunder. Oren released his grip and slapped the deer on the backside. It immediately bolted out of the camp.

I looked over at Alexis. She was in shock.

"That was disappointing!" I said.

"Are you kidding me?" Alexis said. "I could have thrown Bambi on his butt. Is it me, or did Thunder just TOTALLY wuss out?"

"It's not you. Clearly, the mighty Thunder didn't want to be skewered by the antlers of death," I said.

"Thank goodness the Quads weren't here to see that," said Alexis.

As soon as she said it, we both turned and looked at each other. How'd we forget?

THE QUADS! Where could they be? Lost in the woods? Captured by a momma bear?

And to make matters worse, Mr. Odom was one of the security guys who had formed the human shield around Thunder. Alexis needed answers.

"Excuse me, Mr. Odom. Where are the Quinlan Quads?" asked Alexis.

"Who? You mean those kids? I have NO idea," said Mr. Odom matter-of-factly.

"What do you mean, you have no idea? You were

assigned to watch them," said Alexis.

"Hold on. I'm an observer, not a babysitter," Mr. Odom said defensively.

"THUNDER!" screamed Alexis at the top of her voice. "EMERGENCY! I need THUNDER BANKS, NOW!"

That certainly got everyone's attention. Immediately, Thunder and Sid came running over.

"I'm so sorry, Thunder, but YOUR Mr. Odom lost the Quads," accused Alexis.

"W-w-wait a minute. I didn't LOSE anyone," stammered Mr. Odom.

"Larry! Where are the Quads?" asked Thunder.

"To be honest . . . they got away from me," admitted Larry Odom. "But you have NO IDEA how quick those little guys are."

"Seriously, Larry? You're a British commando. You couldn't track four eight-year-olds?" asked Thunder.

Instantly, the scene exploded into a lot of adults pointing fingers and blaming each other for the disappearance of Camp Wild Survival's youngest campers.

That's when I spotted a smiling Barrett Quinlan skipping into camp. He snuck through the crowd and started pulling on Thunder's ergonomic, UV-protected survival trousers.

"WHOA! Who do we have here?" said Thunder as he hoisted Barrett into the air. "Sorry, little man, I don't know which one you are, but I'm happier than a croc in a wallaby's pouch to see ya."

"Barrett!" howled an overly dramatic Alexis. I'm sure she knew the cameras were rolling.

From what I knew about the Quads, Barrett was the brains of the operation. He was sneaky and resourceful, so when I saw him smiling, I knew everything was okay.

"Is it too late, Mr. Banks? Did we make it back in time?" asked Barrett.

"You sure did, mate. Now, where are your brothers?" asked Thunder.

"They're over there, behind your RV. And we have a surprise for you," said Barrett enthusiastically.

"No worries, mate," Thunder said. "I'm just glad you blokes are okay. You gave us quite the scare."

"Scare? You don't have to worry about us. We're survivors. And we can do a lot more than just dig worms," said Barrett, glaring at my dad. "So we decided to go on a REAL hunt!"

"SID! Are you guys getting this? You were right . . . TV GOLD!" shouted Thunder.

Leading the crowd over to the RV, Barrett described the Quads' hunting plan.

"We knew there was BIG GAME in the woods. But we had to be extra quiet. So, sorry, but the first thing we did was get rid of that guy," Barrett said, pointing at Mr. Odom.

"Interesting," Thunder said, glancing over at Larry Odom. "Continue . . ."

"We were scared at first, but then we remembered what you always say: 'There are no rules in survival.' So we went for it!" said Barrett, now jumping up and down.

"EXACTLY!" Thunder declared. "The Quads against the elements! On their own, lost in the deep woods. A classic kill-or-be-killed situation. No room for error. Love it!"

Sid motioned for the camera crew to get ahead of the advancing crowd. He wanted the cameramen to shoot from all angles—and he didn't want them to miss any of the drama.

"So, I'm fascinated. What did our youngest wild

survivors bag on their first solo hunt?" asked Thunder, speaking into the camera.

Barrett raced behind the RV to get his brothers. Even I was curious. Maybe we could still win the challenge? But it had to be something big enough to beat Oren Longboat's angry deer.

Suddenly, the heads of all four Quads peered around the corner of Thunder's massive RV.

"Ready, Thunder?" they asked.

"Absolutely!" he answered.

Popping back behind the luxury house on wheels, the Quads could be heard quietly discussing last-minute details.

Suddenly, Merrett triumphantly appeared, struggling to pull a large rope . . . with an even LARGER dairy cow attached to the other end. And, yes, Jerrett, Barrett, and Gerrett were riding on top of their new pet.

"We present to you . . . Moo-la!" screamed Merrett. "Allegany County's number one milk-producer. Let's EAT!"

After a few seconds of uncomfortable silence, Thunder exploded in laughter.

"Fair dinkum, boys!" howled Thunder. "You Quads RULE!"

"CUT! CUT! CUT!" shouted Sid.

CHAPTER 12
LOOK ME IN THE EYE!

They take cow theft seriously in western Maryland. Moo-la's owner showed up minutes later, crazy mad AND carrying his shotgun. The sheriff wasn't far behind.

Besides the Quads having stolen Farmer Hendersen's prized possession, the biggest problem was that Moo-la wasn't your ordinary farm animal. As an eight-time county milking champ, that heifer was more valuable than most people's cars. Stealing her was

STEP AWAY FROM THE COW.

a FELONY! The Quads could have been looking at ten years in jail. Holy COW!

But, luckily, the Quads were only eight years old. And if Thunder Banks was good for anything, it was laying on the charm.

Fortunately, Farmer Hendersen and Sheriff Baker were big Thunder fans. All he had to do was admit some "errors in judgment" and make a few promises. Toss in a group photo and an autographed DVD collection, and the Quads were free to go.

That afternoon at Tribal Council, where Thunder declared the challenge winner and awarded points, Thunder named Himalaya the winner of the hunting-and-gathering challenge. They were awarded one hundred points for Mr. Longboat's impressive capture of a live deer.

All the tribes were once again asked to stay within the camp's boundaries—and to not break any laws! Thunder then asked the Quads to come forward. The four boys nervously shuffled to the front, probably thinking they were getting kicked out of camp.

But in a surprise move of AWESOMENESS, Thunder announced Tribe Bali Aga had earned fifty Thunder Points for the Quads' outside-the-box thinking. Even though they had technically broken the law, they were pure survivors.

SURVIVAL CHALLENGE SCOREBOARD

FAMILY NAME	TRIBAL NAME	SCORE
DONALD WINSTON AND OREN LONGBOAT	HIMALAYA	100
THE MATHEWSES AND THE QUINLANS	BALI AGA	50
THE BOYDS	PALAU	0
THE ANDREWSES	BIG SUR	0
THE CONLEYS	DENALI	0

f LIKE US ON FACEBOOK 🐦 @ THUNDERBANKS

Instantly, the hyperactive Quads were back in business. "THUNDER! THUNDER! THUNDER!"

Next up was a survival knife lesson. Instructor Dave demonstrated the proper techniques for handling and sharpening a blade, which was necessary for perfect filleting and for preparing a fish for the frying pan.

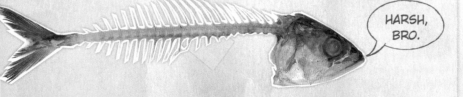

HARSH, BRO.

Dad felt great! Because of our tremendous fishing success, each camper got their own practice fish, and everyone was looking forward to a delicious dinner.

I'm not going to lie, though. The whole blood-and-guts thing FREAKED me out.

Dad, Alexis, and the Quads dove right in and were soon up to their elbows in fish disgustingness.

"Dude! What's the matter?" asked Michael as he professionally filleted his lake trout in record time.

"Sorry, Thunder Jr.!" I said. "I'm just not feelin' it. It seems so mean."

"Come on. You want to eat, don't you?" asked Michael.

"Not really," I said. "I think I agree with DW-All-About-ME. How do we know Black Lake is even clean? It doesn't *sound* clean. They might want to change the name."

Instructor Dave came over and tried to persuade me to cut open my stiff, dead, and smelly friend.

"Gee, Dave. I just don't know where to cut. Can you show me one more time?" I asked.

He wasn't buying what I was trying to sell.

But before I could try to convince Alexis to do my dirty work for me, a mighty hand landed firmly on my shoulder. Turning around, I was blinded by intense lights. It was Thunder and his camera crew.

"Come on, mate! Give it a go!" encouraged Thunder. "Picture this: You've been in the bush for days. You're tired. WEAK! Starving. Your body is screaming, 'FEED ME!' You don't want to die, do ya?"

I don't know if it was the pressure of being filmed, or just the fact that I wanted to get him away from me.

But I agreed with Thunder.
I wanted to LIVE.
Plus, everyone was now
watching me.

At Thunder's urging,
I did the unthinkable.
Guts, grossness, and
fish goop covered
my hands. I wasn't
going to starve after all.
Jake Ali Mathews was a survivor!

JAKE THE
SURVIVOR!

"Excellent job, Jake. Now it's time for Thunder's tip
of the day," he said, grabbing my filleted fish carcass and
turning to the camera.

"In the wild, you never know where your next meal
is going to come from. So NEVER, EVER discard your fish
head. Cut it off, wrap it in leaves, and keep it in your
pocket. Yeah, it's going to smell like an overheated dirty
diaper. But it could save your life in a pinch.

"One time, I was shipwrecked on Tortuga. Starving . . . dehydrated . . . The only food I had was a fish head I stole from a seagull. Without hesitation, I sucked both eyeballs into my mouth. The liquids and essential fatty acids were enough to last me until help arrived."

~Dramatic pause~

"CUT! Really great job, Thunder," said Sid. "Man, your storytelling is getting so much better. And that thoughtful expression? You nailed it!"

"Wow. Thanks, Sid!" Thunder replied. "My acting coach told me I'm improving, but hearing it from you makes all the hard work worth it."

Turning back to my table, Thunder thanked me and Michael for helping with his tip segment.

"Now, I can't promise you boys will be on TV," Thunder said, "but who knows? You guys might be BIG stars."

I looked up to see Alexis and the Quads jealously watching all my "Thunder attention." *Time for some fun.*

"Thank you, Thunder! Excellent tip," I said politely.
"But I am a little confused. How exactly do you suck the
eyeballs out of a fish? Can you demonstrate?"

Reaching over and grabbing Michael's fish head—with
the skeleton body still attached—I handed it to our
fearless host.

Thunder was a real pro. He wasn't going let some kid
make him look bad. Without hesitation he grabbed the fish
head from my hand.

"Absolutely! What was I thinking?" apologized
Thunder. "You know what they say: Give a man a fish,
keep him a couch-loving, fast-food-craving casualty. Teach
a man how to suck the lifesaving goodness out of a fish
eye, turn him into a TRUE survivor for life!"

I'm POSITIVE that's NOT what they say.

"Yes, a demonstration it is. But since I'm fuller than a
centipede's sock drawer, Instructor Dave will gladly show
you how it's done. Right, Dave?" asked Thunder.

I immediately looked over at Alexis. I could see the

disappointment in her eyes. The real Thunder Banks wasn't anything like the guy on TV.

With cameras, lights, and a crowd of campers now focused on Instructor Dave, the poor guy didn't have a choice. He reluctantly took the fish head and quickly sucked out the left eye. After a few chews and a VERY hard swallow, he handed it back to Thunder.

"And there you have it, folks. Easy! Right, Dave?" asked Thunder.

"Yup, easy," answered Dave, who suddenly didn't look very well.

"Once again, in a survival situation, always feed your body and mind. No matter what. Your mission is to LIVE!" urged Thunder. "Now, for one hundred Thunder Points, who'd like to have a go at the right eye?"

Before Alexis and the Quads could take their first steps forward, Michael was out of his chair, standing in front of Thunder. His hand was raised high.

DUDE! Don't do it!

Without hesitation, Michael ate the right eyeball like a champ. Combined with his tribe's one hundred points for winning the knife-skills challenge, there was a new leader at Camp Wild Survival.

GROSS.

SURVIVAL CHALLENGE
SCOREBOARD

FAMILY NAME	TRIBAL NAME	SCORE
THE BOYDS	PALAU	200
DONALD WINSTON AND OREN LONGBOAT	HIMALAYA	100
THE MATHEWSES AND THE QUINLANS	BALI AGA	50
THE ANDREWSES	BIG SUR	0
THE CONLEYS	DENALI	0

LIKE US ON FACEBOOK @THUNDERBANKS

CHAPTER 13
PREPPING FOR
WHAT?

Sitting around a roaring campfire with a plate full of delicious fried lake trout was a perfect ending to our day.

It was fun to finally get to know the other families. The TV cameras were off, and Thunder was busy meeting with Sid and the production team. There was no chance of any more crazy tips or any ridiculous Thunder adventure stories.

The prepper family had a daughter around Alexis's age, so she and the Quads were hanging out over there.

Michael and I talked to Oren Longboat about how he caught his deer, while my dad and Mr. Boyd sat with the doctor couple from DC and chatted.

We were THIS close to getting Oren Longboat to admit he wasn't really related to the Winstons when an annoyed DW III came bounding over.

"There you are. I've been looking all over for you," growled DW III. "Please take me back to the island. I need my sleep."

"Yes, sir," said Oren Longboat, putting down his plate and getting up. "Nice talking to you boys."

"Great talking to you too, sir . . . I mean, Donald's cousin," said Michael.

"Nighty-night, Donald. Don't let the bedbugs bite. Or the mosquitoes. Or the beavers . . . ," I teased.

"Yeah, DW III, beavers have *huge* teeth. They love to gnaw on your ankles while you sleep," said Michael.

OUCH. →

Getting up for more food, we decided to join Alexis and the preppers on the other side of the fire.

"There he is!" shouted Mr. Conley, father of the prepper clan. "It took some guts to eat that fish eye."

"It wasn't that bad. A little salty," said Michael humbly.

"Also, a very smart tactical decision. You and your dad are now in the lead," said Mr. Conley.

"We are? I didn't notice," Michael said with a laugh, pointing his finger in my face.

I knew he was competitive, but come on. Eating a fish eye was next-level disgusting.

"One eye is nothing!" shouted Barrett Quinlan from across the fire. "I would have eaten the whole head."

"Yeah, Barrett!" said Jerrett. "That would have been worth, like, a MILLION Thunder Points."

"That fish head was bigger than you, little man," said

Michael. "I'm not sure you could lift it."

After some friendly taunting, the Quads ran off to play. Those kids had unlimited energy, and Alexis knew they needed to run around more before bedtime.

As we sat around the campfire with Mr. Conley, he explained why he had come to Camp Wild Survival and how the training was perfect for his prepper lifestyle. While trying not to be disrespectful, I attempted to learn more about why he was a prepper.

"Jake, we live in a scary world. And as a father and a husband, it's my job to prepare and protect my family," explained Mr. Conley.

"Yes. But you can't prepare for all uncertainties. Right?" I asked.

"Correct," said Father Prepper.

"I believe something *big* is coming. Something horrible. And when we're finally faced with TEOTWAWKI, the Conleys will be ready."

"TEO-what?" asked Alexis. "I'm sorry, we don't speak Japanese?"

"'TEOTWAWKI' is prepper lingo for 'The End of the World as We Know It,'" Mr. Conley said.

"Cool word!" said Alexis.

"Sounds more like WOMBAT to me," I whispered to Michael.

"Wombat?" asked Michael.

"Waste of Money, Brains, and Time." I laughed.

Knowing I was about to cross the line between curiousness and obnoxious pestering, I still had to ask what exactly he thought was coming. What was this guy prepping for?

"I'd rather keep that private," Mr. Conley said. "But I have an uneasy feeling. Have you ever felt like something bad was about to happen? You can sense it in your gut . . ."

"Yeah . . . ," I answered. "Every time I walk into the locker room. *Is Jason the Jerk going to give me a wedgie?*

Or stuff me in a locker?" I answered. "But you did say something *horrible* was coming. Can I guess?"

"JAKE!" yelled Alexis. "You're being rude."

"No, dear," Mr. Conley said. "It's okay. I love the fact he's interested. I wish more kids took it seriously." He looked over at his daughter and son.

Both of them rolled their eyes and gave a classic *I'm over it* look of teen disgust.

"And I wish I could eat some real food. Something *not* from a can!" Mr. Conley's daughter said. "And I wish we didn't have to sleep in that underground bunker EVERY weekend! And I WISH . . ."

"That's enough, sweetie," Mr. Conley said calmly. "I already know how you feel."

Wow. Trouble in prepper paradise. I had to lighten the mood. "Okay, Mr. Conley. I'm going to try to guess the horror coming soon to a theater near you. READY?" I asked.

"Fire away," said Mr. Conley.

Jake: "Genetically modified apes take over the world?"

Prepper Dad: "No."

Jake: "Alien Invaders from another galaxy?"

PD: "No."

Jake: "Asteroid?"

PD: "No."

Jake: "Artificially intelligent robot uprising?"

PD: "Ummm . . . No."

Jake: "Super volcano!"

PD: "No."

Jake: "Massive flooding caused by the melting of the polar ice caps?"

PD: "No . . . but that's a serious threat."

Jake: "Vampires . . . and not the ones who are all nice and friendly."

PD: "No . . . but close."

Jake: "REALLY?"

"Jake! What are you doing?" asked my dad, who was now standing behind me.

"What? I'm trying to guess TEOTWAWKI," I answered.

Dad scowled. He thought I was being annoying. I didn't agree. But I wasn't in the position to argue with our tribe's leader.

Since we were now in third place, Dad called for a Bali Aga meeting to get ready for the next day's challenges.

Alexis rounded up the Quads, and Bali Aga huddled around Dad.

"All right, guys. We have three challenges left. I think we can win them all," whispered Dad. "But before I go on, raise your hand if you are okay with me still leading the tribe."

"There you go again, *asking* to be the leader," said Alexis.

I quickly raised my hand in support of Dad.

Dad looked over at Alexis and pretended to talk into an imaginary phone. She got the message.

With the Quads waiting to see which way Alexis voted, my older sister slowly raised her hand. That was good enough for the Quads. It was unanimous. Dad was still our tribal chief.

But then our supersecret planning meeting was suddenly disrupted. Dr. Mike Andrews sprinted up the hill, running away from the lake and screaming like a madman. His wife wasn't far behind.

"They're back! The killer bees! I heard them BUZZING!" yelled Dr. Mike.

Thunder, Sid, and the whole camp staff came running to investigate.

"A giant swarm of bees! They're everywhere! Run for your lives!" Dr. Jillian bawled.

"Whoa . . . wait a minute. Settle down, doctors. What exactly did you hear?" asked Thunder.

"The buzz!" Dr. Mike said.

WITH KNIVES LIKE THEEZZZ, WHO NEEDS A STINGER?

"The same loud buzzing we heard the first night. The bees are back, and they're all over the lake."

"You saw them?" asked Sid.

"No. But we heard them. What else could it be? The only things in nature that buzz are ferocious, bloodsucking bees," explained Dr. Mike.

"Bloodsucking? This guy's a doctor, right?" I asked Michael.

Thunder and his team weren't buying it. So everyone in the camp went down to the lake to check it out. I suddenly remembered DW III and Oren Longboat were on the island. Beavers and bees are a BAD combination.

As we slowly approached Black Lake, everything seemed calm and quiet. No sign of anything. There was a nice fire going on Donald Island. Thunder called out to Oren Longboat and DW III.

There was no reply. Then Thunder called out again.

"Yessss? How can I help you?" answered DW III from his island stronghold.

"Did you guys hear anything strange? Dr. Andrews thinks killers bees are in the area," shouted Thunder.

"Preposterous! We didn't hear anything," said DW III. "Just enjoying a nice fish dinner with my cousin. But if I hear ANYTHING, I will report it immediately."

Acting disappointed that there were no killer bees, Thunder and his team headed back to camp. As I walked close behind, I saw Thunder turn to Sid.

"Seems like Doc Andrews has a few *roos* loose in the top paddock, *ay?*" Thunder laughed.

Sid agreed.

I wasn't so sure. I knew DW III didn't eat lake fish. But he must be eating something. What? And what was that buzzing?

CHAPTER 14
THUNDER
POINTS

Over the next two days, Camp Wild Survival turned ultracompetitive. Everyone wanted their tribe on top of the leader board. And there were plenty of Thunder Points for the taking. The more insane and crazy you acted, the more Thunder loved it.

To be VERY honest, it was a LOT more fun than I ever imagined it could be. We were having a blast. The only one not having much fun was Alexis. She hated losing.

The orienteering challenge was especially traumatic for Alexis, because our tribe's last-place finish was all her fault. *Orienteering* is just a fancy word for map-reading.

It seemed simple enough. Each team got a map and a compass, and had to find ten different checkpoints scattered in the woods. The team that did it in the shortest time won.

"Excuse me, Thunder. What's this funny-looking watch thingy?" asked DW III.

"It's a compass," answered Thunder.

"What's it for?" asked DW III.

"Are you kidding? It makes popcorn! What do you think it's for, mate? Directions! It tells you where you're going," lectured Thunder.

"Oh, I get it," DW III said. "Like the GPS in my dad's car. Can I have a talking compass, please? It will make it so much easier."

He didn't get that talking compass, but since he

had Oren Longboat, outdoorsman extraordinaire, Team Himalaya won that challenge easily. We could have beaten them. But Alexis entrusted our only compass to Merrett Quinlan.

Merrett was the "crazy" Quinlan quadruplet. You know, that kid who jumps off the swing set at its highest point and "sleds" down the stairs in a cardboard box. He's completely reckless and not very smart.

As Thunder would say, *"Not enough brains to give himself a headache!"*

So halfway through the challenge (we were winning at that point), Bali Aga stopped by the lake for a rest. Merrett decided to see how many times he could skip our compass across the water. He couldn't resist. It was just too round and flat NOT to try.

With a mighty side-armed chuck, it was on its way. The other three Quads started counting out the skips. "One, two, three, four, five, six, seven, eight, nine . . . ten!"

Afterward, Merrett told us that his plan had been to dive in and find the compass. Unfortunately, Black Lake got its name for a reason: You can't see the bottom.

The next challenge was the mountain run. Each team had to race to the top of Big Savage Mountain. The first team to light their colored signal flare was the winner.

Thunder and his team of advisers were spread out all over the course. They were on the lookout to award Thunder Points to any team that wanted to push its skills to the limit.

Instead of having us run *around* a rugged cliff, Thunder urged the teams to climb straight up and over. What about a steep gorge with fast-moving white water? *Pffft!* Mountain-slide down the side of that sucker and cross the river at its widest, deepest point. Thunder wanted made-for-TV risk-taking and a pure survivor's will to live.

Dad let us know that under NO circumstances would there be ANY risk-taking. Even Merrett Quinlan couldn't believe what he was hearing from Thunder.

But halfway up the mountain, Dad was done. Even though he could flip a tractor tire fifty times, he didn't have mountain-running stamina. Alexis was fuming mad at Dad's lack of fitness.

Thankfully, DW III wasn't in any better shape. He didn't even try to run. And since the winning tribe had to get all its members to the top, Michael and his dad took another one hundred points in a close battle with the doctors.

The final challenge should have been ours. A timed canoe race across Black Lake was perfect for Bali Aga. There were seven of us, including the unlimited energy of Quad power.

All we had to do was keep the canoe straight and paddle home to victory. But Alexis didn't agree with Dad's placement of team members in the boat. She insisted she and the Quads should sit in the back of the canoe, working together like an engine. She wanted Dad and me to sit in the front and steer. Dad said "no way," and Alexis got angry. It was all downhill from there.

We didn't make it twenty yards from shore before our canoe started going around in circles. There was no teamwork. Nobody was listening. It was a complete and utter disaster.

The prepper family easily posted the best time. Evidently, an emergency canoe was part of their "bug-out plan" and they practiced nonstop each weekend. But it was also becoming apparent that Dad was failing as our tribe's leader.

Five days in the woods with six kids was taking its toll on the Big Guy. He looked tired and beaten.

That night at Tribal Council, we saw the updated

scoreboard. At least we weren't in last place.

SURVIVAL CHALLENGE SCOREBOARD

FAMILY NAME	TRIBAL NAME	SCORE
THE BOYDS	PALAU	300
DONALD WINSTON AND OREN LONGBOAT	HIMALAYA	200
THE CONLEYS	DENALI	100
THE MATHEWSES AND THE QUINLANS	BALI AGA	50
THE ANDREWSES	BIG SUR	0

LIKE US ON FACEBOOK   @ THUNDERBANKS

Alexis was at her competitive breaking point. She couldn't handle losing and asked Thunder for permission to quit Tribe Bali Aga.

Thunder and his staff said okay, and Alexis and the Quads immediately joined the preppers and Tribe Denali.

Thunder then stood up with a major announcement:

"All right, campers. First, I'm impressed. You guys are killing it out there," Thunder said. "But now it's time to put what you've learned to the ultimate test. Your last challenge—a winner-take-all survival battle."

Everyone got real quiet. Alexis glared over at me and Dad and gave us a slash-the-throat gesture. *Easy! Remember, we're your REAL family.*

"I call this the Apex Predator Showdown: tribe versus tribe in a no-rules, survival-of the fittest game of capture the flag."

"Excuse me, Thunder," interrupted Dr. Mike. "When you say *no rules*, what exactly do you mean?"

"Anything goes, mate. You're trying to win, right?" asked Thunder. "And survival is winning. Are there any rules in a life-or-death situation?"

"Hold on. Sorry, allow me to jump in here," said Sid. "Of course there are *rules*. What Thunder is saying is let's *also* respect the other teams and be good sports."

"NO! That's not what I'm saying at all, SID! I don't see

your name on the camp brochure," lectured Thunder.

"Can we capture and torture the other campers?" asked Merrett Quinlan.

"YESSSSS!" screamed Thunder.

"NO! Of course not," answered Sid. "Everyone, give us five. Obviously, we need to iron out some of the details."

Thunder, Sid, and several other staff members started to argue with each other outside the tent.

"So, what do you think?" asked Dad.

"I don't know. Maybe we can win?" I said.

"No. The whole Camp Wild Survival thing?" asked Dad. "Are you having fun?"

"I'm having a GREAT time!" I said.

"Awesome. I'm so glad we did this," said Dad. "It's a little embarrassing, though. I guess I don't know as much about 'survival' as I thought."

"No problem," I said. "Who knew you could eat fish eyes? Or that cutting open and climbing inside a dead musk ox can provide lifesaving shelter in the middle of a glacier!"

We both laughed hysterically. About 99 percent of the stuff we'd learned that week was a total waste of time. But, boy, it sure was entertaining.

"What's so funny, you two?" asked Alexis, now standing over us with the Quads at her side.

"I'm sorry. Remember, it's now tribe versus tribe. If I tell you what's funny, I'm going to have to kill you," I said, laughing louder.

"Don't worry, Jake. You can tell me. We're BACK with Tribe Bali Aga!" announced Alexis.

"Why? I mean, what happened, sweetheart?" asked Dad. "You didn't like your new prepper papa?"

"*Yuck!* NO WAY! I can't team up with a guy who is prepping for the zombie apocalypse!"

said Alexis. "I'd be the laughingstock of the survival community."

"ZOMBIES! That was my next guess!" I screamed. "I knew it!"

Dad welcomed Alexis and the Quads back into the tribe.

Since it was late, and Thunder and Sid were still arguing, we all headed back to our shelter for some sleep. Apex Predator Showdown was going to be tough. And Bali Aga needed to rest up.

CHAPTER 15
I'M OUT!

Waking up to a bright, sunny mountain morning, I felt PRETTY good. Sure, living outside wasn't great, but we had a good shelter and a warm fire. What more could you ask for?

"Coffee! I need coffee!" moaned Dad.

Truth be told, Dad looked worse. He could barely move. His back was acting up, and he hadn't gotten much sleep. His caffeine withdrawal must have been awful.

MUST . . . HAVE . . . COFFEE!

Why do you think there's a coffee shop on every street corner in America? Because our parents are hooked on caffeine. And when you take it away from them, they get weak and CRANKY!

Adding to his survival misery were the freaky sleep-talking Quads, who had kept Dad up all night. Apparently, the brothers have the bizarre ability to share dreams while they sleep. That night it had been all about panda bears and giant cupcakes.

"Oh yeah, they do that ALL the time! So weird!" said Alexis.

As we slowly walked to Tribal Council, Dad was falling farther and farther behind.

"How many more days of this?" asked Dad.

"Two," I said. "Don't worry, you can do it. We got this!"

"I don't know, Jake," said Dad. "This isn't fun anymore. I'm starving. I'm miserable. I can't really run. Especially up a mountain! We've lost most of the challenges because of me. And Alexis and the Quads aren't listening."

"Come on! You're doing great. Who cares if we're not in the lead? Our tribe can still win the final challenge!" I said, trying to boost his spirits.

But there was no rallying him. To make matters worse, as we got closer to base camp, you could smell the morning breakfast being prepared for Team Thunder.

"Those lucky ducks!" Alexis exclaimed as she sniffed the air. "Nothing like the smell of bacon and eggs in the morning. Right, Dad?"

Dad just put his head down and kept marching.

Thunder was standing on the yellow base-camp line, greeting all the tribes with a hearty "G'day!" In his right hand was a giant bagel filled with cream cheese.

I don't even think it crossed his mind what a jerk move it was to stand there eating in front of us. Thunder was totally clueless. Remember, it was HIS name on the camp brochure.

Looking over and drooling at the sight of the buffet,

Dad tiredly called for me and Alexis.

"Announcement time, kids!" he said. "That's it. This is the end of the road for me."

"What are you talking about, Dad?" I asked.

"See that cozy cabin over there next to Thunder's RV? It's got my name on it. Sorry, Jake. I just can't do it anymore. It's been fun! But I'm more of a 'Monday-morning armchair survivalist' who is nowhere near as tough as he thought," admitted Dad.

"You're quitting?" asked a stunned Alexis. "Does this mean I'm in charge?"

"HOLD ON!" I yelled. "Dad, are you sure you want to do this? We need you."

"Ah, you don't need me. I'm just holding you back," said Dad. "Alexis, I officially pass the leadership torch of Tribe Bali Aga to you. DON'T abuse your power. And be nice to your brother."

"YEAH! About TIME!" screamed Alexis as she ran off to tell the brothers.

Dad slipped off his backpack and tossed me his multipurpose tool.

"Listen. I am *so* proud of you, Jake. You did *way* better than me this week," said Dad. "But it's easier to have Alexis in charge. If not, she'll just fight you at every step."

We hugged it out, and Dad signaled to Team Thunder that he was done. *Get that man some coffee.*

"Hey, Dad!" I yelled as he was running toward the cafeteria tent.

"What?" he shouted.

"I can't wait to tell Mom *you're* the one who quit!" I laughed.

Joining Alexis and the Quads inside, we didn't have to wait long to receive the Apex Predator Showdown rules update. Basically, just like Thunder wanted, there were no rules.

"As I already mentioned, this is the final challenge. The ultimate test!" said Thunder. "Each team will be given a flag with your tribe's name on it. Protect that flag at all times. And stay within the boundaries of the camp. Those are the rules."

Sid was standing outside the tent with his arms crossed, looking very disappointed. Obviously, the Thunder tantrum had been too much to overcome.

Thunder took questions from the campers and went into a little more detail about the event. Basically you could do anything to capture another team's flag. Stealing, raiding, trickery, scheming, sabotage . . . you know, the usual! But each team had to openly display their flag at all times (no hiding it under a rock), and the last tribe holding their own flag was the winner.

"And, trust me, you're going to want to win. I can't tell you what the grand prize is, but if you're into survival and the outdoors, you're going to LOVE IT!" Thunder assured us.

The Quads were going absolutely BONKERS! They were like little kids waiting to be turned loose on their Christmas presents. The thought of what the grand prize could possibly be was driving each of them crazy with anticipation.

But Alexis just nodded her head. Long gone was the Thunder fangirl who hung on her idol's every word. No longer did she worship every craggy rock face he rappelled down or his absurd stories of life-or-death situations . . . where he miraculously ALWAYS came out like a conquering hero.

"Oh, golly gosh, what could the grand prize be, Alexis? Maybe a hand-carved Amazonian blowgun with a lifetime supply of poisoned darts?" I asked.

"Yeah, but I'm sure it would be a cheap plastic FAKE.

Just like him," Alexis said with a sneer. "But I still want to win, so I can tell Thunder exactly what he can do with his stupid prize and EXACTLY what I think about his RV, his bodyguards, and this made-for-TV camp."

OUCH! Finally, Alexis had seen the light. I had been wondering how long it would take for her to admit this guy and his "survival" training was a complete joke.

But I was also glad to see she still wanted to win. And if there was anyone who would completely embrace the no-rules aspect of the Apex Predator Showdown, it was MY big sister.

Look out, other tribes. Alexis the Terrible is in the house. Hide your flags! And any snacks or candy you might have. IT'S ... ABOUT ... TO ... GO ... DOWN!

CHAPTER 16
CRASH AND BURN

With a mighty blast from Thunder's favorite (and most annoying) air horn, the five tribes sprinted across the yellow line separating base camp from the lawless great outdoors.

It was like a giant game of hide-and-seek. Each team had one hour to hide and prepare for the coming battle. When Thunder blasted the horn again, that signaled the start of the Apex Predator Showdown.

Alexis wasted no time in establishing her leadership. Unlike Dad, she didn't ask.

"Here's the deal. We're going to WIN. There is no way

any of these losers are going to capture this flag," Alexis said, holding our flag high over her head and whipping the Quads into a frenzy.

"*Shhhhhh!* Hold on! Settle down, Coach," I whispered. "You don't want the other teams to know where we are, do you?"

I'M SSOO SCARED.

"Jake, Jake, Jake . . . as usual, you've got it all wrong," lectured Alexis. "You're thinking like a scared little rabbit. You want to run and hide in your hole, *hoping* the Big Bad Wolf doesn't gobble you up!"

"Yeah, Jake, you're a frightened bunny," yelled Barrett Quinlan.

Yes! That's exactly what I was thinking: *Let's hide in the woods and lay low for a few days, and maybe everyone else will quit.* Sounded like a plan to me.

"Little bro. We ARE the Big Bad Wolf!" declared Alexis. "We're not hiding from anyone. Bali Aga is the hunter, NOT the hunted."

The Quads immediately started to crawl around on all fours, snarl, and howl like wolf pups. Alexis loved it. She was born to play Apex Predator Showdown.

Suddenly, a second air-horn blast snapped everyone back to reality. Putting on her most serious game face, Alexis looked around at her tribe and confidently whispered, "Let's do this!"

First order of business was to make sure we didn't have to

worry about of the "survival" stuff. Jogging north toward the entrance of camp, we found the spot where Alexis had hidden her giant green garbage bag filled with supplies.

Grabbing two pop-up tents, matches, a few boxes of gummy bears, and enough energy drinks to power a small country, Bali Aga headed back to Black Lake.

Finally setting up camp high on a hill, Alexis picked out the perfect spot. We could see everything going on below, and there was no way another tribe could sneak up on us from behind.

Looking off into the distance across the lake, I laughed when I noticed the smoke rising from Donald Island. Alexis shielded her eyes from the sun and noticed it, too.

"Good. DW III is first to go," snarled Alexis.

"Really? How are we going to get him off the island?" I asked.

"We don't need to," Alexis assured me. "We're going to make him quit. Sorry, Donald, no delivery for you tonight, Mr. Fancy-Pants!"

Okaaay! But before I could ask what the heck she was talking about, Alexis ordered everyone to get ready. We were moving out. Time to hunt.

Descending quickly from our elevated campsite, Bali Aga was again back in the thick woods. This time we beelined it south, directly toward base camp. Maneuvering our way through the trees and prickly bushes, we ended up right behind Thunder's RV and the old wooden buildings.

"What are we doing?" I finally asked.

"*Shhhhh!* Be quiet," whispered Alexis. "We need to get some more supplies."

Barrett and Alexis got into a serious discussion.

"Are you sure? The one on the left side is the right storage shed?" Alexis asked, pointing to the little building.

"I'm positive. When we were riding Moo-la, I looked in the window," said Barrett. "The place is FULL of them."

"Okay, Quads!" Alexis said. "You guys know what to do. We'll meet you at the door."

The Quads darted out of the bushes, running in

formation, rolling, and jumping like four highly trained mini ninja warriors.

Immediately they formed a Quad pyramid against the side of the shed. Merrett scrambled to the top and started to work on the window. Sliding it open, he pulled himself up and dropped out of sight. Within seconds, the front door opened and the rest of us rushed inside.

Alexis found the light switch. *WHOA! Not what I expected.*

"YES!" shouted Alexis, doing a little dance. We were surrounded by racks and racks of paintball guns, helmets, protective masks, and ammo. Since my dad took us to play paintball every year, I knew exactly how much those things hurt. I was Alexis's favorite target.

"Remember, Jake, 'no rules,'" Alexis whispered with a smile.

We loaded up. Now Tribe Bali Aga ACTUALLY looked like we were going to war.

With the sun going down, Alexis led us back through the woods to the lake. We moved swiftly and silently, heading straight toward Donald Island.

But I have to admit, I was confused. The island was about thirty yards offshore. And there was no way to capture Donald's flag from where we were standing.

"This is stupid. We can't get at him from here. How are you going to make him quit?" I asked Alexis.

"Patience, little bro," said Alexis. "We're not hunting DW III. We're hunting his killer bees!"

Alexis and the Quads all laughed.

MAN, I hate being on the outside of an inside joke. What the heck were they talking about? I didn't have to wait long to find out.

All of a sudden, the Quads started pointing and jumping up and down in excitement. Alexis started looking around. Then I heard it: a strange buzzing sound, getting louder and louder. It was coming toward us.

"Merrett, Jerrett, and Gerrett, you guys go over there behind that big log," instructed Alexis.

Grabbing me and Barrett, she led the way to the edge of the lake, where we positioned ourselves right in front of the island.

"When I give the signal, BLAST IT!" screamed Alexis.

Then out of the corner of my eye, I spotted DW III emerging from his supervillain island lair. He walked to the top of a big rock, carefully scanning the lake, looking for something.

As the buzzing grew louder, Alexis smacked me on the arm.

"Look!" she said, pointing up in the sky. I couldn't believe what I saw.

Out of nowhere, a tiny drone helicopter appeared and began hovering over Donald Island. It was carrying what looked like pizza boxes and a six-pack of soda. The strange-looking aircraft slowly started to descend. DW

III stood underneath, waving and
guiding the drone down
to his position.

"FIRE!" commanded Alexis.

The POP, POP, POP, POP, POP, POP
of six paintball guns filled the air,
causing a terrified DW
III to almost fall off his
rock and into the lake.

Within feet of
successfully delivering its delicious cargo, the buzzing
drone started to take some direct hits. Clouds of
multicolored paint rained down on Donald, who was now
jumping up and down, wildly trying to grab his dinner.

"Noooooooooo!" he screamed as we continued our
assault. *Splat! Splat! Splat!*

A few more well-placed shots and it was
OVER. The drone started to smoke and tilt
to the side. Out of control and out of power,

the expensive toy veered sharply toward the shore and crashed at our feet.

Twisted and broken, the drone's onboard camera stared up at us as Bali Aga huddled around to investigate the futuristic pizza deliveryman.

"Hi, Mrs. Winston!" announced Alexis, bending down and putting her face right in the camera.

"Sorry about your drone. But we're in the middle of the Apex Predator Showdown. Hope you don't mind. This lake is a no-drone zone. Pizza delivery is forbidden!"

"I HATE YOU!" screamed Donald as he tumbled into his canoe and Oren Longboat slowly paddled them to shore.

Picking up the broken drone and pointing its camera toward Donald, Alexis went in for the breaking-news interview.

"This is Alexis Mathews, reporting LIVE from Black Lake—site of a horrible drone accident," mocked Alexis as she pushed the camera closer to Donald's face.

"I'm DONE. Mom, come get me!" screamed Donald, looking into the drone's camera, hoping the microphone still worked. Frustrated and furious, DW III threw down the Tribe Himalaya flag and stormed back to base camp.

Being a friend of the environment and overall AWESOME dude, Oren Longboat went back and cleared the island of all the leftover pizza boxes and soda cans. He said good-bye and wished us the best of luck.

Bali Aga was off to a great start. One tribe down, three to go. And amazingly, the extra-large pizza survived the crash with its crazy cheesy crust still intact. We ate well that night.

CHAPTER 17
WATCH YOUR BACK

The next morning, Alexis asked me to hike to base camp to check out the leader board.

She really wanted to go herself but didn't trust the Quads with guarding our flag. With their extremely short attention spans, a cool-looking bush or an especially pillowy cloud was all it would take to distract the brothers.

I didn't mind the long walk. It was GREAT to get away from the tribe. Sure, Alexis was a decent leader. But she had to know everything that was going on. Even my bathroom breaks were met with *where, when, why,* and *how*?

Arriving at the Tribal Council, I was proud to see
Himalaya crossed off. And I wasn't shocked Big Sur was
also gone.

SURVIVAL CHALLENGE SCOREBOARD

FAMILY NAME	TRIBAL NAME	SCORE
THE BOYDS	PALAU	300
DONALD WINSTON AND OREN LONGBOAT	HIMALAYA	200
THE CONLEYS	DENALI	100
THE MATHEWSES AND THE QUINLANS	BALI AGA	50
THE ANDREWSES	BIG SUR	0

LIKE US ON FACEBOOK   @ THUNDERBANKS

"They really didn't put up much of a fight," said
Michael, seemingly coming out of nowhere.

I shrieked like my mom does when she sees a spider in
the kitchen.

"Holy geez, MAN! What are you doing?" I yelled at Michael. My spastic overreaction couldn't be unseen.

"Don't worry, Jake, you're in a safe place," Michael said with a laugh as he walked toward me. "I don't see your flag. Obviously, you don't have it. Or do you?"

Michael made a fake aggressive charge. But instead, he grabbed a folding chair and sat down. I did the same.

Maybe it was a trap? I quickly scanned the tent for his dad . . . or some kind of human leg snare? Nothing.

"Did you guys really shoot down DW III's pizza drone?" asked Michael.

"Yeah. It was AWESOME. And once he realized his pizza pipeline was closed, he quit immediately," I said.

"Same thing with Big Sur," said Michael. "It was SO weird. Dad and I were just walking along, and the two doctors popped out of the woods right in front of us. They didn't even try to run. They just handed us their flag and screamed, 'We surrender!'"

After a good laugh and an awkward silence that

seemed to last minutes, it was time for me get to moving.

"SOOOO! And NOW there were three," I said, getting up slowly, still not totally trusting my best friend. Could this all be part of an elaborate kidnapping plot? Sadly, I knew Alexis would never pay to get me back.

"What's your problem, Mr. Paranoid?" asked Michael.

"NOT paranoid. Just cautious," I said, backing out of the tent.

"All right, crazy dude. Good luck. I'll see you out there," said Michael.

"Not if I see you first!" I said eerily, imagining I was the hero in a blockbuster spy movie where former best friends now had to fight against each in order to save the earth. Michael looked confused.

*Note to self: dramatic movie reenactment
scenes don't work unless all participants
know exactly what is going on in your head.*

Quickly looking over at the cafeteria tent, I didn't see Dad. No big deal. I'm sure he was probably playing Xbox with Thunder in his RV or something like that.

I suddenly heard a very loud *PSST*. It was coming from behind the boathouse.

"*PSST!*" There it was again. I decided to ignore it. Could be a trap.

"Hey, Jake! Get over here!" yelled Larry Odom, looking very annoyed.

"What do YOU want?" I asked, not getting too close.

"I have something for Alexis. It's a note from Thunder," said Larry. "He asked me to give it to you."

"Aren't you a little old to be passing notes, Larry?" I questioned.

"Funny! Just take it so I can get back to the buffet line. The pancakes have been disappearing really quickly since your dad showed up," added Larry.

"Why is Thunder sending Alexis a note? Did every tribe get a note?" I asked.

"I don't know. What do I look like, Thunder's secretary?" asked Larry.

"Yes, that's exactly what you look like," I said.

"Come on. Just take it. Maybe they want you guys to win? I don't know. You're kids. The Quads are funny. It's all good TV," said Larry.

I snatched the note from his hand, looking around nervously. I expected a giant net to be thrown over me.

On my walk back to Alexis and the Quads, I REALLY wanted to read the note. But I knew Alexis would freak out. She hated when I read her text messages. And this was a supersecret letter from THE Thunder Banks. Better not. She had a paintball gun and wasn't afraid to use it.

Strolling into camp, I saw Alexis sitting alone by the

fire, the Bali Aga flag proudly planted in the ground next to her. But no Quads.

"It's now down to three tribes," I said, sitting down, exhausted from the hike up the hill.

"Let me guess: us, Wild Boy/Wild Dad, and the nutso preppers," said Alexis.

"Exactly!" I said. "So, where are the boys? Doing a little hunting for horses? Goats? Or other defenseless farm animals?"

"No. They're getting ready for our next attack," said Alexis. "You'll see. Trust me, it's perfect."

"Okaaaay!" I said, enjoying the peace and quiet around camp. But I was feeling a little like DW III, who let Oren Longboat take care of everything. Unfortunately, I didn't have Mr. Longboat in my tribe. I was entrusting our success to my overemotional sister—who happened to believe in dragons—and eight-year-old quadruplets who thought cow hunting was a good idea.

"Oh yeah, special delivery! Here's a note from your

secret admirer," I said, tossing Alexis the note.

From the way she jumped back and rolled out of the way, you'd think I'd just passed her an angry rattlesnake.

"What, are you crazy!" screamed Alexis.

"CRAZY? You wrote the book," I said. "It's not a BOMB! It's a note from Thunder."

"How do you know? It could be a tracking device. You led the enemy right to our doorstep!" screamed Alexis.

Okay! Someone needed to breathe. *It's just a GAME.*

"Can I open it? And prove to you it's just a note?" I asked. Alexis nodded.

Hmmm. How thoughtful! A nice note AND a detailed map?

Dear Alexis and Tribe Bali Aga,

Excellent use of paintball guns! I couldn't be prouder. Just want you to know the Thunder Points are piling up for Bali Aga.

But the game isn't over yet. Here's a map that you might find useful. Remember, there

are NO RULES in Apex Predator Showdown.
And just one winner!

Destroy this note after reading it!

THUNDER

"What a MORON! I don't need his help!" shouted
Alexis. She quickly studied the detailed map, before
handing it to me. "I ALREADY know where they're both
hiding. Burn that note before the Quads get back. It will
just hurt their feelings."

I wasn't too sure. So I committed the map to memory
before crumpling it up and chucking it in the fire. You
NEVER know. Alexis had been wrong before.

CHAPTER 18
THE WALKING DEAD

On the morning of the seventh day of Camp Wild Survival, everyone was eager to win and get home.

How many Meathead Tires sales had I missed? I NEEDED my computer! I heard the *click, click, click* of my keyboard and the warm-up music of my smartphone in my dreams.

Come back, Jake!

First order of business was taking care of crazy prepper dad. Alexis knew exactly where Mr. Conley and his kids were camped, so she figured they would be the easiest to eliminate.

Remember, Bali Aga was the hunter, not the hunted.

The plan was simple: Don't waste energy trying to steal his flag when psychological warfare was much easier. What did prepper dad fear most? *Exactly.*

But in order to pull off our Apex Predator Showdown scare tactic, we needed the perfect zombie.

Even though the Quinlan Quads are four identical quadruplets, they couldn't be more different in personality.

Barrett was a scheming smarty who was always on the lookout for ways to make money and beat the system. That's why he was my favorite. I saw a bright future for that young man. Merrett was a crazy risk-taker. Jerrett was the quiet one and the best athlete. He usually did exactly what Barrett told him to do. And then there was Gerrett—my LEAST favorite Quad.

Gerrett was the funny guy—actor, comedian, and king prankster. If all the alarms in the house were mysteriously reset to 4:30 a.m., it was Gerrett. If a cookie's vanilla filling had been replaced with toothpaste, Gerrett had struck again.

You know the type: ANNOYING! And he never admitted anything—always staying in "falsely accused" character and defending his innocence to the end. Of course, Alexis thought he was the GREATEST.

It didn't take that long to transform Gerrett Quinlan into a decent-looking zombie, even though we were in the middle of nowhere. You can do some amazing things with milkweed, charcoal, and sumac berries.

And after the other Quads happily tore apart his shirt and pants, Gerrett looked just like any other ordinary member of the walking dead. He had a ghostly pale face, giant dark circles under his eyes, and tons of "blood" coming out of his mouth and nose. Scary stuff.

We all watched from the woods as Gerrett—bent over, head tilted, and moaning exactly like a hungry zombie— masterfully shuffled into Mr. Conley's campsite. And that was all it took.

"RUUN!" screamed Mr. Conley at the first sight of the kid zombie. Tripping over his backpack and jumping over his sleeping son, prepper dad sprinted into the woods without looking back.

Laughing uncontrollably, Mr. Conley's teenage daughter happily handed Gerrett their flag and thanked him for a "great job." *One down, one to go.*

With no time to celebrate our zombie victory, Bali Aga quickly cleaned up our own campsite and prepared for the final battle.

On our way to turn in the Denali flag at the Tribal Council, Alexis explained her plan for defeating Michael and his father.

Since Palau was the strongest, most experienced tribe, the only way we could win was through "divide and conquer." We had to separate the father-son duo and then go after their flag with all our might.

"How are we going to do that?" I asked.

"Mr. Boyd is a former Army Ranger! This isn't his first survival rodeo."

"That may be true, but I bet he's never been stuck in quicksand before," said Alexis, turning to high-five each one of the Quads.

"He's going down, Jake!" screamed crazy Merrett.

"'Help me! I'm Mr. Boyd. I've fallen, and I can't get up,'" mocked Gerrett.

The four brothers spontaneously erupted into whoops like a gang of psyched-up loonies. Alexis was right in the middle, playing the role of hype man.

Alexis: "Who's better than Bali Aga?"

Quads: "Nobody!"

Alexis: "C'mon now, I CAN'T HEAR YOU!"

Quads: "NOBODY!"

Alexis: "Are we going to WIN?"

Quads: "YEAH!"

Alexis: "I said, are we going to WIN?"

Quads: "YEAAAHHHHHHHH!"

Alexis and the Quads:

"I believe that we can win!

I believe that we can win!

I believe that we can win!"

Once again, I was on the outside, looking into the very bizarre world of Alexis and her Quads.

Passing out the last of our Cyclone Energy drinks and PowerBars, our tribe's leader prepared us for the final showdown.

CHAPTER 19
BEWARE OF
QUICKSAND

It was no surprise that everyone at base camp heard us coming. Passing over the yellow boundary line, I saw Dad, Thunder, Sid, and many of the instructors ready to greet us. Alexis was having none of it. The game wasn't over yet. Bali Aga still had a lot of work to do.

After viciously driving the Denali flagpole into the ground of the Tribal Council tent, Alexis quickly turned around and headed out to find Palau.

But Alexis didn't count on my dad running out of the tent and giving her a big hug and kiss. It kind of ruined her tough-guy moment. "Okaaaay, Dad. Thank you! You can let go of me now. I'll see ya later!"

Thanks to Thunder's cheat map, Alexis's hunch that Michael and his dad were camping in the hills south of Black Lake was confirmed. It made sense. There were plenty of places to hide, there was access to freshwater, and it was not too far from base camp.

"Okay, guys, here's the plan," said Alexis. "We're going to walk in there and take Palau's flag."

The Quads roared with excitement. I wasn't too sure.

"*That's* the plan?" I asked. "Just walk into the woods, find Michael and his dad, and hope they just stand there and let you take their flag? Brilliant! Why didn't I think of that?"

"Because you're dumb," said Alexis. "Remember, it's just you, me, and four eight-year-olds. They're going to expect something sneaky. Something 'outside the Thunder box.' But we're not going to give it to them."

"We're not going to GIVE IT TO THEM, JAKE!" yelled Gerrett. "No, sir!"

"In their minds, they're the big, tough schoolyard bully. And Bali Aga is the little wimp. So I suggest we just go right up to karate boy and Captain America, and punch them right in the nose," Alexis said.

"*Hoo-hah!* That's right. Sock 'em one right in the nose," echoed Merrett. "AND take their lunch money!"

"We can't punch them!" I protested.

"Come on, Jake! It's a metaphor, man! I thought you took advanced classes!" Barrett said.

Watch it, kid! You're my favorite, don't push it.

After Alexis explained her plan in detail, I had to admit, it was kind of smart. It's not like Mr. Boyd was going to have a tug-of-war with a bunch of kids over a flag. He's an adult. The flag-protection and flag-capturing duties would be Michael's responsibility.

All we had to do was separate Michael from his father, and the Palau flag was ours for the taking.

I still had my doubts about Alexis's plan, but I was very surprised to see her first prediction come true.

Michael and his dad certainly weren't expecting our aggressive attack. As soon as we walked into the woods on the south side of the lake, we saw Tribe Palau right there, a few hundred feet up the hill. It looked like they were having lunch.

They were INDEED shocked to see us.

We stormed the Hill like raiding pirates, screaming and blasting the father-son team. I stayed in the back, carrying our flag. I just didn't feel right shooting my best friend and his dad with paintballs. They were unarmed, and those things REALLY sting.

As we closed in on their position, Alexis was right again. Michael grabbed their flag and bolted out of sight, leaving his father behind.

You could tell Mr. Boyd was impressed. Sure, he took a few paintball hits, but he loved our coordination and aggressive frontal assault. Alexis called out, "Hold your fire!" as we surrounded the former Army Ranger.

"Great job, kids. I honestly didn't see that coming.

Sorry to have underestimated you," apologized Mr. Boyd.

"That's okay," said Alexis. "I'd love to stick around and chat, but I have a flag to capture. Quads, make sure Mr. Boyd doesn't follow us. And please don't hurt him. Jake, you're with me."

Before Michael's dad could even turn around to see what was coming, the brothers were on him. And when I say "on him," I literally mean crawling all over him. Mr. Boyd had stepped into Quad Quicksand. There was no escape.

I know what you're thinking: *The Quads are little kids. How could they hold down a grown man?* The simple answer is they couldn't. They don't try to hold you down. What they do is wear you out. Remember, there are four of them. One for each limb.

Merrett quickly ducked in and latched on to Mr. Boyd's right leg. Barrett grabbed the left. And when Mr. Boyd bent over to try to yank one off, Gerrett wrapped himself around his left arm and Jerrett around his right.

No matter how big and strong you are, it is nearly impossible to move with a sixty-pound eight-year-old stuck like glue to each of your arms and legs. Even if you're lucky enough to get one loose, these kids are like army ants. In a flash, they're back on, holding tighter than before.

You might even be able to walk a few feet. Mr. Boyd did. But eventually, the extra 240 pounds of Quinlan brothers will weigh you down, until it feels like your whole body is sinking to the ground. That's Quad Quicksand.

I tried desperately to keep up with Alexis, but she was in midseason lacrosse form. Her daily speed and agility training was really paying off. Bursting through some bushes, we stumbled into a clearing. Ahead of us, Michael was still awkwardly trying to hold his flag up high as he struggled toward the top of the steepening slope.

Once she had him in her sights, Alexis snorted like a crazed rodeo bull and charged up the hill. Michael might have been a champion martial-arts guy, but that didn't mean he could outrun my sister.

Gasping for breath and barely moving, Michael was out of gas and out of luck. Alexis was on him in seconds. The hunter captured her prey and easily yanked the flag from his hand.

Racing past me with the Palau flag in her teeth, Alexis gave me a thumbs-up and headed straight down the hill, back in the direction of base camp.

When I eventually reached Michael's— and his tribe's—final resting place, I looked down at my exhausted best friend.

"Wow! You are in TERRIBLE shape," I said, extending my hand and pulling Michael up to his feet.

"She's . . . fast . . . couldn't . . . so fast!" struggled Michael, sounding like he was about to have a heart attack.

"It's okay, buddy," I said. "I live with it every day. Just try to breathe. We can't have you passing out."

Taking it real slow down the hill, I tried to make Michael feel a little better.

"You know, you guys were the last tribe. And definitely the hardest to get," I said.

"Shut up, jerk!" gasped Michael. "You know what this means!"

I did. Alexis was NEVER going to let Michael forget she had crushed him in Apex Predator Showdown. It was something he'd have to live with forever.

CHAPTER 20
GRAB THE MIC

Once Alexis delivered the Palau flag to the Tribal Council, the game was over.

But there was no relaxing. Base camp frantically buzzed with the planning and production of the final awards ceremony.

It was Thunder's big moment, where he would declare the winner of the Apex Predator Showdown and unveil the grand prize.

I just wanted to pack up and go home. But Alexis clearly had other thoughts. This was what she'd waited for all week—the perfect chance to tell her fallen idol exactly what she now thought of him.

Before we even got a chance to
eat or talk to my dad, Tribe Bali Aga
was hustled off to hair and makeup.
We had to look our best, because
TV cameras would be rolling, and
there would be interviews and group
pictures. All the stuff I hate.

But the Quads were LOVING
hair and makeup. Surprisingly, they
were VERY particular about their
appearance.

I'M READY FOR
MY CLOSE-UP.

After a brief Quad huddle, Barrett informed the
makeup artist all four of them would be requiring tribal-
warrior face paint. Sid said, "No way," but Thunder
thought it was the best idea ever. That took an extra
thirty minutes. Thanks, guys!

The camp staff built a little stage in front of Thunder's
RV, which was quickly surrounded by lights, microphones,

and cameras. Right in front of the stage was a gigantic teleprompter with THUNDER written in tape under the screen.

I sat with Alexis and the Quads in the greenroom off to the side of the stage. Peeking outside the tent, I saw Thunder nervously rehearsing his lines. Tapping Alexis on the shoulder, I motioned for her to check it out.

"Here's your chance," I said. "Thunder's right outside. Tell him what you think so we can get out of here."

"Are you kidding? No thanks. I'll wait until I'm onstage before I detonate my humiliation bomb," said Alexis. "It's going to be a drop-the-mic moment people will never forget."

I knew my sister was hard-core, but I could see this getting really ugly.

Suddenly, loud classical music filled the tent, and we could hear Thunder welcoming everyone. Man, that guy could talk. It felt like an hour before a production assistant stuck his head into our tent and shouted, "Thirty seconds!"

Tribe Bali Aga then lined up and took the stage, led by Merrett Quinlan, who proudly held up his index finger, declaring that we were number one.

I saw Dad, Michael, and Mr. Boyd sitting right in the front. Sid had a headset on and was screaming instructions, and Thunder stood in the middle of the stage. Everyone clapped as we were introduced one by one. I have to admit, it was really cool.

"Apex Predator Showdown was a survival battle of the fittest. A true journey of discovery to find the warrior within," announced Thunder. "And I can't tell everyone how proud I am that our youngest tribe turned out to be our fiercest."

The Quads reacted just as expected: by whooping, screaming, and pointing at themselves and then at Thunder. The tribal face paint was perfect. Alexis looked bored. But

I knew this was the calm before the verbal storm.

"Alexis, come on out here," said Thunder. "Ladies and gentlemen, Alexis Mathews, leader of Tribe Bali Aga."

Fixing her hair and smiling for the crowd and the cameras, Alexis strolled up and stood at Thunder's side.

"Like I said before, congratulations on winning Apex Predator Showdown. You guys were incredible," praised Thunder. "How do you feel about the victory?"

"It was very tough, but SO worth it!" said Alexis with big fake smile. "I get the chance to stand next to you, on this stage, AND SAY—"

"Oh, sweetheart! You get WAY more than just a chance to stand next little ole me." Thunder laughed. "Let me tell you what you won!"

Before Alexis could grab the microphone back, one of Thunder's staff jumped onstage and handed each of us a framed Camp Wild Survival diploma.

"First, each member of Bali Aga takes home a five-hundred-dollar gift certificate from ThunderBanks.com," announced Thunder. "That's RIGHT! From knives to tents, to monoculars to multi-tools, everything the modern-day survivalist is looking for can be found at THUNDERBANKS.com."

Alexis looked back at me with her classic *I told you so* face.

"What do you think of that, young lady?" asked an excited Thunder Banks.

"Yeah? Cool. Thank you," said a frustrated Alexis. "But like I was saying, it's great to have this opportunity to finally tell YOU—"

"What? How much Camp Wild Survival changed your life?" asked Thunder.

"YES!" screamed the Quads all at once. No longer able to control themselves, they mobbed Thunder and Alexis. Sid motioned for me to join the celebration.

"CRIKEY. This reminds me of the time I was surrounded by tribesmen in Mongolia!" screamed Thunder, loving every minute of it.

"BUT! An incredibly valuable gift certificate isn't all you get," announced Thunder. "There's MUCH MORE."

Visibly shaking, looking like a volcano about to explode, Alexis tried one more time to gain control of the mic. But it wasn't happening. Thunder didn't like to share the spotlight with anyone.

"How would you guys like to join ME for an all-expenses-paid luxury weekend in New York City?" asked Thunder.

For the first time, the Quads were silenced. Alexis quickly turned to Thunder, looking for confirmation of what he had just said. *New York City? Luxury?*

"I talking private jet, five-diamond hotel accommodations, the finest restaurants, AND an appearance on the red carpet at the premiere of my new show, *Thunder Banks vs. Mother Nature.*"

Suddenly, to my great surprise, Thunder handed Alexis the mic and awaited her response.

"Thunder Banks, YOU, SIR, are the GREATEST!" screamed Alexis.

Pandemonium ensued. Quads were leaping, Alexis was hugging, confetti was dropping, and the cameras captured every moment.

I slipped offstage to finally talk to Dad and the Boyds. "Awesome job, Jake," said Dad. "I'm so proud of you."

"Thanks. I couldn't have done it without you," I said,

giving the Big Guy a BIG hug.

Suddenly the craziness of the award ceremony was brought to an abrupt halt by the distinct sound of an approaching helicopter. A REAL helicopter.

Grabbing the microphone one last time, Thunder addressed the audience.

"In Thunder Banks tradition, I always leave a survival challenge ALIVE and with a bird's-eye view of the terrain I just conquered. Today is no different," said Thunder. "Bali Aga, you guys are with me!"

Sid approached my dad and asked for permission for the helicopter to take us back to Ellicott City. They had already called Mom, and she was ready to pick us up at the local airport.

Alexis, Thunder, and the Quads now surrounded my dad, waiting for his answer.

"Why not? You guys earned it!" announced Dad.

"*Bewdy!*" shouted Thunder as he turned to lead Bali Aga in a sprint to the waiting chopper. I decided to stay behind with Dad and the Boyds.

"Are you sure, Jake? Looks like fun," asked Dad.

"Absolutely," I said. "The long ride home is going to be the best part."

Alexis and the Quads took a quick selfie with Thunder before climbing into the helicopter and putting on some cool-looking headphones.  Thunder stepped halfway through the still-open sliding door, while keeping his other foot on the skid as the helicopter began to hover. A cameraman stood just below him capturing this—his signature move. He then delivered his final Thunder Tip:

"Mother Nature is a beautiful provider. BUT cross her or underestimate her power, and the mighty Earth Mother will make you pay the ultimate price. Camp Wild Survival is all about living in the 'NOW' on your journey of self-discovery. Because inside all of us is a savage survivor, willing to do whatever it takes to get home! Stay safe . . . and STAY ALIVE!"

Thunder then slapped the side of the helicopter, signaling to the pilot it was time to go.

As they rapidly rose up out of the camp, I swear I saw Thunder reach into his pocket, pull out his phone, and take another selfie while still leaning out of the helicopter.

"That's not necessary. He's going to get himself killed!" screamed Mr. Boyd, shielding his eyes from the dust and wind.

True. It was a stupid stunt. But it was PURE Thunder, living in the "NOW," and desperately hoping the TV cameras were still rolling.

I looked forward to the long, SAFE drive home.

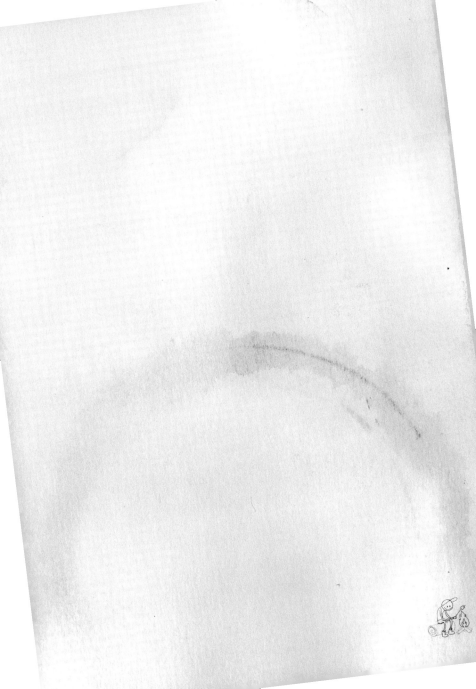

ABOUT THE AWESOME AUTHOR

Jake Marcionette is a ninth-grader living with his mom, dad, and big sister in Florida. He wrote the manuscript for *Just Jake* when he was just twelve years old. His first book debuted at #7 on the *New York Times* Best Seller List. In addition to writing, Jake loves playing lacrosse and annoying his sister, Alexis. You can learn more about Jake at www.justjake.com.